# THE ALIEN EMISSARY

### Interspecies Alliances: Book 1

---

## ERYN IVERS

Cover Design by: Cormar Covers

Editing by: Rascon Revisions

## Chapter One

BRYANT DID NOT DO BURGLARIES. He was always the muscle. He showed up and looked menacing and roughed people up if that didn't do the trick. The closest he came to burgling was the occasional stickup at the docks, and the workers there were so used to it they just handed everything over without batting an eye.

But Bryant was very much in a beggars-can't-be-choosers situation. And that wasn't just because he was currently huddled under a tattered blanket, panhandling with an old exhaust pipe. He was watching the Qeshian ship across the hangar from him. He needed to hit it, fence his loot, and take his earnings to the police station—all in under three station hours. Astrid, the clever girl, was the one who had first spotted it, so it was fitting that it should provide her bail.

Assuming Bryant could pull this off.

Astrid had had her eye on it ever since it came in. She wasn't a burglar either—tended to follow more in his physical-solution-to-everything footsteps—but she was resourceful, and this ship had stood out to her.

1

It was the personal ship of a Qeshian emissary, sleek and high-end but on the smaller side for the representative of the wealthiest species state in the galaxy. And not very well guarded from what they'd seen. But they hadn't seen all that much. They hadn't cased it or asked anyone else to. Bryant had barely had time to ask around about it this morning. A job like this would have required a month or more, and the ship was due to leave today. Bryant would have preferred to just let it go. It wasn't worth the risk.

Or at least, it hadn't been.

"Buy yourself something pretty."

Bryant looked up as a small, clinking pouch dropped into the mutilated exhaust pipe. He caught the eye of the well-dressed gentlemen who'd dropped it and exchanged a tiny nod before pulling the pouch toward him. Buried in the nuts and bolts that had given the bag its heft was a crumpled piece of paper with a series of numbers scrawled across it. Roger could be a cold, greedy bastard, but he was damn effective.

Bryant peered through the crowd flowing over the main hangar thoroughfare to the Qeshian ship. This Emissary Serihk might like his ship on the small side, but Bryant had no doubt it was filled with luxury, and Bryant only needed one piece of it. Roger had a black-market buyer desperate for Qeshian ivory, and he'd pay handsomely for the smallest of trinkets. And small was what Bryant was after, because too many guards were stalking through the fancy hangar for him to get away with dragging a bag full of loot out of a ship like that.

What gave Bryant hope was that there didn't seem to be any guards on the ship itself. The emissary's only security personnel was the hulking klah'eel bodyguard who accompanied him on his business about the station. Non-security personnel were limited to a handful of servants, most of whom were out preparing for their departure that evening. This meant the ship usually sat empty.

As Bryant expected it to be in approximately ten station minutes.

So, for ten minutes, Bryant watched the ship and tried not to think about why he was there. He tried not to think about his thirteen-year-old daughter sitting in a holding cell or the penal colony transport that would dock in three hours to take her and every other unlucky criminal nobody still locked up.

He gritted his teeth. It wouldn't happen. He would make sure of it. He would get Astrid out.

And when he got her out, he would get them both—or at the very least, her—off this station. She'd lost Devin's latest supply of drugs, which meant Bryant either managed to scrounge up even *more* money to pay him off, or they ran. A penal colony was bad, but Devin might be worse.

Bryant tore his mind away from his dismal thoughts as Emissary Serihk appeared at the front door of his ship, right on schedule. The stereotypically long and elegant qesh strode down the gangway, the ends of his robe fluttering behind him. Turquoise shimmered along his pale cheekbones and up to his temples in that ever-changing way of the qesh. It reminded Bryant of the sea creatures he sometimes saw in barrels and tanks at the wet markets on Carta, but much more beautiful. He looked so self-assured, Bryant felt a surprising pulse of resentment. It must be nice to be rich and powerful and from a species state that wasn't a corrupt, broken piece of shit.

The emissary's giant klah'eel bodyguard followed just behind him. Her arms rippled with muscle, and her tusks looked like she must file them daily to keep them so pointed and sharp. Big as Bryant was, he was glad he wouldn't be tangling with her.

Just one housemaid to go, and he'd be clear.

As soon as he glimpsed the mousy-haired girl scurrying away, Bryant shed his tattered blanket and quickly made his way to the ship's side entrance. In the relative safety of the shadow of the ship and its neighbor, he pulled out a set of slim tools from his pocket. After a brief glance around, he set to work jury-rigging the door so he could input the door codes but bypass the biometrics. He wasn't a good burglar, but he'd lived on the streets long enough to know the basics.

Within a minute, he tapped in the last digit, and the door slid open with a soft hiss. Before he could rethink, Bryant slipped inside and closed the door behind him.

The interior of the Qeshian ship was as posh as Bryant had expected, despite its subtle exterior. Soft rugs lined the floors, and furniture made of dark hard wood filled the rooms. A passenger could be fooled into thinking they were in a planet-side manor if not for the curious lack of windows.

Bryant rolled his shoulders. Just find one ivory trinket. In and out.

He hurried through the hallways, not bothering to be quiet. He was no good at it. He passed a few bedrooms, but none looked particularly promising, and he didn't have the time to rummage through drawers.

Despite the still and empty ship, Bryant couldn't shake a creeping sense of unease. On any other job, he would have trusted his gut and gone back the way he came in. But Astrid didn't have time for that, and so he pushed forward. He'd always been good at ignoring the tangle of fear that lived forever in his belly.

After a few more unpromising doors, the hallway opened up into the entrance hall. He stopped. His eyes lit on a large, prominently displayed candelabra carved from solid ivory. His mouth dropped open, but he discarded the option quickly. That wasn't small at all.

Instead, Bryant focused his attention on a carved, decorative dagger sitting on a bookshelf beside leather-bound tomes. The tiny, fragile thing must be worth a fortune.

He took a deep breath and stole across the empty space to the bookshelf. He chewed on his lip as he stared at the thing, hardly daring to touch it. He couldn't see any triggers or cameras. Nothing to indicate that the dagger wasn't just sitting there, ready to be taken. He swallowed. He'd gotten this far. Before his gut could convince him to do otherwise, Bryant reached out and grasped the dagger.

As he pulled his hand back, a long, thin flex metal tendril shot out from the wall behind the bookshelf and wrapped around his wrist.

Shit.

Bryant tore his arm away from the loose grip and, clutching the dagger to his chest, sprinted back the way he'd come. Another autonomous rope suddenly looped firmly around his calf, and Bryant fell to the plush carpet with a shout. He struggled back to his feet, clawing over the ground, but more and more ropes wrapped around his arms, his chest, his feet, until all hope of escape evaporated. The metallic tentacles dragged him to his knees in the middle of the foyer and pulled his arms so far back he could feel the strain in his shoulders.

Bryant twisted and fought, but when the pain in his joints was too much, he went limp. He dropped his chin to his chest. The thin tendrils pried his fingers apart, and he relinquished his hold on the dagger. It dropped with a soft thud onto the carpet.

Bryant knelt on the floor, panting as the pain eased up. What the hell had just happened?

Lifting his head and glancing around, Bryant saw

dozens of flex metal tentacles of varying lengths and thicknesses extending out from the molding on the wall. He had heard of flex metal—software-controlled appendages hard as steel and as flexible as rubber—but it was a new technology. He'd thought it was primarily used in factories. The scale and complexity of the system now rendering him completely immobile were shocking.

That brought on a new thought that made Bryant shiver. If the Qeshian emissary had invested this much into his security system, maybe he'd also installed neural connections. If he hadn't, the tentacles were impossible to control dynamically. So, upon his discovery, the emissary would probably just call the authorities if they hadn't already been alerted. That was bad. But if he *had* installed a neural link and had done it well, the tentacles would respond to his every thought, even possibly subconscious ones. Depending on the emissary's response to a would-be thief, that could mean beating, tearing off limbs, or violent death. And that would be worse.

Despite himself, Bryant's eyes stung.

He had failed.

The magnitude of that inescapable fact sunk in as he sat trapped on the floor. He tried to shove down the rising panic in his chest. Panicking wouldn't help him out of this situation, it would just fuck him over more. But Bryant wasn't sure he could be much more fucked. He flexed against the metal wrapped around his arms, but that just emphasized how powerless he was.

In just three hours, the penal colony transport ship would dock, and Astrid would be dragged onto it. She would be shipped away to an ice moon and—

Something surprisingly gentle stroked down his cheek.

Bryant jerked back. He stared at the softly swaying

tentacle. As Bryant watched, it reached for him again. He yanked away, and the others tightened their grips.

"What are you…" Bryant trailed off as the smooth metal caressed his face firmly.

Then it and two others pushed into his hair, brushing it back from his face, and massaged his scalp.

"Oh." Bryant's eyes dropped closed. He didn't even have enough give to lean away from the touches. He couldn't do anything but close his eyes while the flex metal pressed and pushed at the knots in his neck and base of his skull.

They tangled into his hair and pulled it lightly, tilting his head this way and that.

Bryant let out a breathy gasp when they pressed into a particularly tight spot on his neck.

"God, that's good," he whispered, letting his head drop to the side to give them more access to the knot.

Gradually, more flex metal tendrils and appendages joined in. They dug into his shoulders, finding knots and attacking them, rubbed up and down his sides, and kneaded the muscles in his legs and arms.

Bryant twisted a few times, checking how firmly he was held, and every time he failed to move, a strange relaxation soothed down his spine.

His situation was no better. Everything in his life was a disaster. But there was nothing—he pulled again at his wrists—nothing he could do about it. The flex metal just kept pushing at him, massaging, kneading, and always stopping on just the right side of painful.

Bryant wondered if this was all the system would do. Loosen him up, relax him, perhaps make him more pliant for interrogation? Then a tentacle brushed under the hem of his shirt.

Bryant's breath caught.

A second, third, and fourth tentacle joined, the smooth metal cool against his skin as they worked under his shirt. He squirmed as they raked it up his sides.

"What—" Bryant choked when one slender tentacle pulled at a nipple.

It teased and rubbed at his small bud until it stood hard and erect. Another tentacle began on his other nipple while the first continued its assault until Bryant whimpered with every new touch. God, it almost hurt. No one had ever done that to him. Partners squeezed his pecs to feel the power there; they didn't tease his nipples until he sobbed. He didn't think he'd ever let them. But the tentacles weren't giving him a choice, and he loved it.

"Oh fuck, yes," he hissed. The overstimulation enthralled Bryant so much, he didn't notice the thin appendages creeping below the waist band of his pants until one brushed the cleft of his ass.

Bryant inhaled sharply and jerked.

For once, the tentacles took notice. They wrapped around Bryant's body and pulled him up from his kneeling position until he had completely left the ground, held aloft by the strong tangle of flex metal. They lifted his arms above his head long enough to pull off his shirt, then tightly secured them behind his back again.

He sighed softly in relief as he hung suspended in the air, his mind fuzzing over in a way it never had before. When the two insistent tentacles finally lost interest in his nipples, a new swarm began creeping and wandering up his legs.

When they reached mid-thigh, Bryant saw something that sent a sudden jolt of awareness through him, that cut through the new fuzzy feeling. A tall, lean figure stood in the shadows of the hallway.

"Hey!" Bryant called. "Who—"

A sharp pinch to his nipple distracted him as a thicker flex metal appendage took advantage of his gasp to thrust into his mouth. Bryant moaned, and it pushed deeper until it nudged the back of his throat.

He had an audience. He had an audience, and the knowledge of that laid a hot shame over the fuzziness creeping back in, even as he was turned away, hiding the figure from sight.

The tentacles pulled off his pants and let them drop to the floor beside his shirt and the dagger. Bryant whined around the tentacle in his mouth when he felt a tug at his underwear. His erection bobbed up as his underwear slid over his hips, and he squeezed his eyes shut in a shame that just made him harder.

The tentacles paused as his underwear hit the floor, leaving him naked and exposed, aloft in the foyer.

Bryant didn't think he'd ever been so hard in his life.

Thin tendrils wound their way around his cock and began jerking him slowly. Oh god, they were so gentle, and they pulled him so sweetly, the flex metal warm from the heat of his own body. Bryant moaned around the metal in his mouth.

The others, too many for Bryant to track in his addling brain, traced across his skin. They trailed over the muscles in his chest, fluttered along his inner thighs, and wound around his balls. Bryant groaned as they pinched and pulled at the skin of his sack.

A thin one slid along the cleft of his ass again, and his breath hitched. They would go that far? As though in answer, the tentacles spread his ass cheeks and positioned him so that his rear faced the hallway. He shuddered as he thought of his tight pucker displayed for the perusal of the man in the shadows.

Cool flex metal ran over his hole, and it twitched.

Bryant moaned as he imagined the show he was putting on. The tentacle did it again and circled his entrance, teasing, making him whine. Bryant nodded frantically, as much as the tentacle in his mouth allowed. He wanted that penetration. He wanted to feel something inside him, and he was so hard, he'd beg for it if he could.

Bryant was far enough gone that he would have let it take him dry, but then another tentacle slid into his mouth next to the first. He sucked enthusiastically on it, on them both, laving up and down with his tongue. A firm stroke from the base of his cock to the tip rewarded his efforts, and Bryant redoubled them with a soft moan. He slicked the appendages as much as saliva could, and before too long, the second one pulled out.

It wasted no time in sliding down his crack to probe at his entrance. The touch of the metal made him twitch again. He squeezed his eyes shut and distracted himself from the inevitable pain by sucking gamely on the tentacle still moving in his mouth, earning a few more firm pulls on his cock.

The slick tendril at his opening pressed inside him, and Bryant grunted. It worked itself in and then out, over and over. It twisted around inside him and pulled at his rim. It pressed and stroked at places no one had ever touched before and set him quivering. It felt so fucking good.

Another tentacle as thin as the other pushed inside of him as well, and together they began stretching him methodically. They stretched so patiently and so slowly that Bryant didn't even register a burn, just the strange erotic combination of intrusion and shame.

And the eyes on him.

Two thick tentacles wrapped around each of his thighs and pulled them apart. Bryant knew with absolute certainty that his voyeur watched with rapt attention as his technology worked him open. And that turned Bryant on more than he knew he could be.

The two tendrils curled, and Bryant jolted and gave a strangled cry. They tapped and rubbed his prostate in turns. Suddenly, it wasn't enough. The tentacle wrapped around his cock wasn't enough. The ones fondling his sack, playing with his prostate, toying with his rim weren't enough. He needed more. It was so much, too much, but god. God, he needed more.

Bryant twisted and whimpered. He tried to twitch his hips, either to chase more friction or impale himself on more tentacle—he didn't care. But Bryant couldn't get the leverage, couldn't move satisfyingly enough. He had to take what he was given. He sucked with renewed vigor and moaned like a slut when metal hit the back of his throat.

The tentacles in his ass halted their assault on his prostate and pulled out, and Bryant let out a sob, drool dripping down his chin and the tentacle in his mouth. His muscles clenched around nothing, winking his hole at the man in the hallway. But before Bryant could cry again in protest, something bigger and colder nudged at his entrance. Slowly, the well-endowed appendage, not yet warm from his body heat, pushed in. It burned slightly, but Bryant was beyond caring. He tried to push back to get more, but the tentacles holding him aloft only tightened their grip to keep him completely still.

So it entered him millimeter by millimeter, pushing into somewhere he'd never let another go. And then finally it was in. Bryant groaned as it pulled out again, dragging along his nerve endings, and his muscles sagged at the flood of pleasure. As his body adjusted to the tentacle's girth, the flex metal warmed to his body heat.

And then it thrust. It thrust slow and deep and steady. His rim stretched and clenched obscenely, and with his legs spread wide, he could only envision the display he made, and it felt so good. The tentacle in his mouth changed to match the rhythm of the one in his ass, and they fucked him from both ends.

The thick appendage rubbed over his prostate, and Bryant keened.

The contraption began in earnest at this signal, both tentacles speeding up to a brutal, *perfect* pace. Bryant bounced between them with each thrust so sweetly, so thoroughly violated. The tentacle in his ass hit his prostate with mechanical precision, driving him up and up to indescribable, painful pleasure.

Tears formed in Bryant's eyes. Wanton moans and curses and sobs fell around the tentacle he sucked in a near-constant stream. His entire body burned with overwhelming pleasure.

Finally, a thin, thin tentacle probed into the slit of his cock, and Bryant came uncontrollably.

The force of his orgasm shocked him, and his vision blacked out. He felt himself coming and coming, felt some of his spunk splatter onto his stomach. Every nerve in his body screamed, crying out as the tentacle milked his prostate through his orgasm until he sobbed with the overstimulation. Then it slid out, leaving him empty. They unwrapped from around his cock and balls and gently, so gently, laid him, quivering, onto the plush carpet.

Bryant lay there, panting and shaking. He should move. He needed to move. He couldn't sit there vulnerable, he knew this. But he didn't have the willpower. His entire being was still languid and relaxed in a way he had never been in his life. And the carpet felt so soft against his bare, sweaty skin.

The flex metal tentacles pulled into the wall as though they'd never been there, and soft footsteps approached where Bryant lay, outside his field of vision. Long, slender fingers threaded through and pushed back the sweaty hair at his temple. Smooth, cool skin, not metal.

"My name is Serihk," said a deep, melodic voice in Universal. "It's a pleasure to meet you."

The fingers carded across his scalp again, lulling Bryant. His mind started to agitate for fighting or fleeing, but it was muted, and his body was simply too sated to care. He blinked slowly and turned his head to face the man who had his hand in Bryant's hair. Emissary Serihk looked down at him with his fathomless black eyes and a slight smile on his pretty lips. A rich purple swirled up his neck, over his jaw, and reached for his temples. Bryant had heard that the colors and patterns on a qesh's skin could tell you what they were thinking, but Bryant didn't have a clue. His orgasm-addled mind thought it looked oddly lovely.

Serihk stroked his thumb over Bryant's cheekbone, and Bryant's eyes fluttered closed. The caress soothed him, brought him down gently, and made his heart clench in a painful way that was too poignant to think about. Serihk did it a few more times, and then Bryant heard him stand.

He opened his eyes and watched as Emissary Serihk set the dagger back in its original spot, and it occurred to Bryant that he was lucky it was not buried in his throat. The qesh fixed his black eyes on Bryant with a gaze Bryant couldn't read any more than he could read the slowly eddying swirls of purple over his cheekbones.

Then Serihk glided to the display that had first caught Bryant's eye and picked up the breathtaking ivory candelabra. He returned to Bryant, knelt, and set it down beside him. Bryant's eyes widened. The qesh looked at him for a few moments and then sighed softly.

"Unfortunately, work beckons." He stood and walked

back to the hallway Bryant knew led to an exit, and Bryant managed to twist his exhausted body enough to keep an eye on him. Before disappearing down its length, Serihk set a hand on the wall and looked back at Bryant with a sly smile. "But please, if you ever find yourself *wanting* for anything else, just knock on the front door."

## Chapter Two

BRYANT LISTENED to the sound of Serihk's footsteps fading away as he caught his breath. After a few moments of silence, dread seeped back into his bones. His chest tightened again and his palms became clammy. He stared at the candelabra sitting an arm's length away. The damn thing was as good as a warrant for his arrest. He'd be lucky to get it out of the hangar, and even Roger would think twice about moving it.

He sat up, wincing as the muscles in his lower back twinged after the unusual exercise. He glanced at the dagger sitting on the shelf and wished he could exchange them, but he didn't dare. Emissary Serihk had dealt with him unusually and—in a way—kindly, but Bryant wasn't going to push it. For whatever reason, the qesh had decided to give him this and not that.

And Bryant didn't have time to waffle. Roger would take it. He'd have to. He'd pay a pittance for it, but it'd be enough.

The candelabra didn't fit all the way into the bag Bryant had brought, so he stuck it halfway in and wrapped his jacket around the rest. He pulled on his clothes and flinched at the feel of the cloth settling over his sticky spend, which was still smeared around his cock and on his stomach. Then he grabbed his bundle and made for the door he'd come in by.

He paused before leaving. He wanted to leave the thing here. He wanted to leave it so badly.

Maybe Rask would give him the money. He could turn on Devin's operation and tell Rask everything he knew and work for him instead. Rask and Devin had been rivals for as long as Bryant had known them. But Rask would get a better deal by turning him back over to Devin for a reward and a little goodwill. There was no gang war right now, and no one wanted a traitor.

This damn thing was what he had. This damn thing and less than three hours to offload it.

He left the ship before his fear could paralyze him any longer.

He walked faster than he should have through the hangar, but he made it out.

Then he made it through the central transport hub.

Three blocks from Roger's shop, when he thought maybe he'd really make it all the way, his luck ran out. Bryant rounded a corner and found himself face-to-face with three station police officers. He froze. The officer in front of him froze with his cigarette halfway to his lips. The officer's gaze flicked down to Bryant's coat tucked against his chest.

Bryant turned on his heel and walked back the way he came.

"Hold on a second, sir."

Bryant broke into a run.

"Stop!"

Bryant had never seen police officers in this neighborhood; they couldn't possibly know it as well as he did. He could lose them around a couple of corners, circle back around, and duck into Roger's. They'd seen his face, but only for a second. They wouldn't remember it, and if they did, that was fine. He just needed to stay free for long enough to get Astrid and get out of here.

He turned another corner and barreled down an alley-way. This was exactly where he needed to be. He just had to take this right—

Bryant's breath left him in a whoosh, and his back slammed into the ground.

"Stay down! Don't move!"

Bryant blinked the stars from his vision to see an officer standing over him with a gun trained on his chest. As Bryant opened his hands and spread his arms, another officer swung into the alley after him. He skidded to a stop when he saw Bryant on the ground and caught his breath before striding over.

"What have you got there?" The officer grabbed the bundle that had fallen to Bryant's side. The fabric of Bryant's coat slipped off as the officer lifted it to reveal the exquisitely carved ivory. "Holy shit."

"It was given to me." Even as the words left Bryant's mouth, he could have kicked himself. No one was going to believe that in a million years. And they definitely weren't going to believe it after he'd made a run for it. He might as well have saved himself the embarrassment.

"Yeah. Sure. You're coming with us."

Bryant let himself be flipped over, and cold metal tightened around his wrists for the second time that day. It didn't feel near as good.

The jail wasn't far. It was conveniently situated in the refugee-dominated wing of the station—where Bryant and everyone he knew holed up—to make it easier to lock up the riffraff. And with the speed of the intra-station trans-port, Bryant only had a few minutes to wrestle down his panic so he could think about what to do next. This wasn't over yet. He had options.

He was being taken to the same jail Astrid was held in, and it only had the one holding cell, which meant they would be together. That was something. But bail was now officially off the table, so Bryant's only hope was to strike a deal with someone. He just had to figure out who and what to offer them.

But when he was shoved into the communal holding cell, any makings of any idea he had were wiped from his mind at the sight of Astrid's pale face.

"Dad!" She leaped from her corner and pushed through the crowd to throw herself against his chest.

"Astrid." Bryant wrapped his arms around her and put his chin on her head. "You're okay. I got you."

"They knew the drop point. They were waiting for me." She leaned back and looked up at him, her eyes a little puffy. "They were waiting for *me*, Dad."

Cold understanding trickled down Bryant's spine. He should have fucking known. The bastard had too many officers on payroll for one of his runs to be busted by acci-dent. Bryant closed his eyes with a growl and tightened his arms around his daughter.

"It was Devin."

"Yeah." Astrid extricated herself and tugged on his arm to lead him to the corner she'd been sitting in. "So, why are you here? Didn't you go ask him for help?"

"No." Bryant planted himself next to her and cast a wary eye over the other criminals in the holding cell. They all eyed him back, but none looked to be hankering for a fight. "I thought you'd just lost him twenty thousand cred-its. I didn't think he'd help, and I didn't have time to try."

"He must have thought you'd come straight to him." Astrid sat on the ground and pulled her knees up to her chest. She looked very small and young like that. She *was* very small and young, and it was only Bryant's complete failure as a father that had gotten her locked up in jail for drug smuggling. "He doesn't want you to leave."

"I know." Bryant crossed his arms and leaned against the wall. He had given Devin eight years of his life as payment for smuggling him and Astrid out of the squalid Carta refugee camp. Lewis Station wasn't much better, but at least he hadn't had to worry so much about his young daughter being kidnapped and trafficked. Those eight years were due to come up this month.

Astrid looked up at him. "What did you do instead?"

"I needed to get your bail, so I hit that Qeshian ship you've been eyeing."

"Yeah?" Astrid perked up and then grimaced. "Oh. And got caught."

"Something like that." A pleasant and inappropriate swoop attacked his lower belly at the memory. His thir-teen-year-old daughter didn't need any more details than that.

"Bryant Harrison." Bryant and Astrid looked up at the paunchy and bored-looking guard at the gate who held a baton in his right hand. "Bryant Harrison, you need to come with me."

Astrid grabbed his wrist, and Bryant squeezed her hand.

"It's gonna be okay," he said, and years of telling her that while privately worrying the exact opposite made the lie roll off his tongue easily. "I'll be back."

She nodded, still young enough to believe him, and let his wrist go. Bryant gave her a small smile and met the guard at the gate.

"Hands through the bars," he ordered and cuffed Bryant again before letting him out.

Bryant saw Astrid flinch when the door slammed shut behind him.

"This way."

The guard led Bryant through the windowless hallways to a door. Without a word of explanation, he opened it and shoved him inside.

Bryant felt only the briefest flicker of surprise when he saw Devin lounging in a chair at the interrogation table. The lanky man's wide mouth spread into a shit-eating grin that made Bryant's blood boil.

"Bryant. So glad I could get to you before that penal colony ship docked," Devin said. He was the best liar Bryant had ever met, so the overt bullshit in his words was deliberate. "And to Astrid. How is she? You know, I can't believe you didn't come to me first."

"I bet you can't," Bryant growled.

Devin chuckled and let the pretense fall off. He leaned back in his chair and crossed his arms. "Well, I think we both know what happens now, don't we? Let's not drag it out."

"I'll give you two more years."

"Five." Devin shook his head and lifted a finger to wag at him. "You're not in a position to negotiate."

"Seven, and you get no claim on Astrid."

That got Devin's attention, and he raised his eyebrows. "Seven and Astrid only works for me for the first two."

Bryant narrowed his eyes. He didn't want to go back to working for this man, and he didn't want Astrid working for him at all. But what was the point of making a deal if Devin had already demonstrated his willingness to play dirty? Bryant had to get Astrid out first. Devin wanted *him*. Astrid was useful but mostly as a tool to keep Bryant in line. If he could get Astrid clear before Devin started worrying about losing Bryant, then maybe she'd be out of his reach by the time Bryant's end date came up again.

Bryant was about to open his mouth to counter one more time when the door opened. The station captain stuck his head in, a tall man with a square jaw that Bryant had only ever seen in passing or on the occasional news screen doing a press briefing.

"Bryant Harrison, you need to come with me."

Bryant's eyes widened.

"We're still busy here," Devin snapped, standing up.

But the captain just shook his head. "Too bad," he said. "Someone a lot more important than you is asking for him."

"What?" Devin gaped.

Bryant didn't blame him. He almost asked who, but it didn't matter. Anyone was better than Devin.

"Now," the captain said, and Bryant shuffled after him, leaving Devin dumbstruck in the interrogation room. He almost flipped him off as he went, but there was no guarantee Bryant wouldn't need him afterward, so he restrained himself.

"You are either a very lucky man, Harrison, or a very unlucky one," the captain said as he led him through the station.

"I always seem to be one of the two," Bryant muttered.

They stepped over a threshold dividing shiny linoleum from stained carpet, leaving the interrogation rooms and heading into the nicer part of the station. *Nice* being a relative term when applied to an underfunded public institution in the shit part of a Human station. Bryant had heard Qeshian and Klah'Eel stations were better, but the Human economy was garbage, and it showed up everywhere.

They came to a hall lined with offices, and Bryant

almost stopped dead at the sight of a familiar klah'eel bodyguard. She stood outside one of the doors, one hand on her hip and the other loosely holding a staff tipped with a wicked-looking serrated blade. Her nostrils flared when Bryant came close, and Bryant barely contained a grimace. The klah'eel sense of smell was legendary, and he was suddenly hyperaware of the dried cum getting crusty in his pubic hair. She narrowed her eyes, but she didn't say anything, and then used the hand that wasn't holding her weapon to open the door for them.

A surprising cascade of emotions hit Bryant at the sight of the tall, elegant figure standing beside the dingy metal desk. Surprise, relief, apprehension, attraction all fell over one another and gathered somewhere in his throat.

Emissary Serihk stood with his hands clasped behind his back, dark green stripes over his jaw and down his neck, and he swept his imperious gaze over Bryant from head to toe. Then he snapped it to the captain.

"Why is he cuffed?" he demanded, then continued before the captain could stutter out a reply. "Release him and return his property to him immediately."

"It-It's in evidence."

"Then retrieve it."

The captain backed quickly for the door, but Serihk's voice snapped out like a whip.

"The cuffs first."

"Right." The captain fumbled the keys but managed to get the cuffs off Bryant's wrists. Bryant didn't blame him. He wouldn't want to be on the other end of that tongue-lashing either. The man fled the room as soon as he'd freed Bryant, leaving Bryant alone with the Qeshian emissary.

Bryant rubbed his wrists and looked up at the qesh slowly. This was the most powerful man Bryant had ever been in a room with. Authority ran through every line of his body. He held himself with confidence and a surety worlds away from the hair-trigger insecurity of the crime bosses Bryant had always known.

The sight of him and the memory of less than an hour ago made something excited fizz and rejoice in Bryant's chest. He had the sudden, ridiculous urge to drop to his knees and rest his forehead on the man's thigh. He wanted to feel the man's long fingers in his hair again. He wanted to let *him* decide what happened now. Emissary Serihk seemed like a man that always knew what to do, and Bryant never did. He just stumbled around from barely scraping by here to barely scraping by there.

But Bryant only let that thought get away from him for a moment before he yanked it back in. No one was going to save him. He'd learned that a long time ago. He would save himself. But he did need this man to do it, and he couldn't blow this opportunity.

"I'm sorry for all this inconvenience," Serihk said, inclining his head. "I should have given you a deed of sale or a written notice of my gift."

"It—" Bryant's tongue felt awkward and clumsy, just like the rest of him around this beautiful man. He had to pull himself together. "It was generous enough already."

Serihk's lips quirked in an almost conspiratorial smile, and the edges of the green lines on his skin tinged purple. "Compared to what I received, I'm not so sure."

A blush blossomed on Bryant's cheeks as arousal pulsed in his lower belly, but he ignored them both to focus on the opening that gave him. He steeled himself and took a step closer to the qesh. For the first time, he wished he had learned the arts of charm and seduction. He'd seen it work for other people, but his bulk and obviously once-broken nose had always inclined him toward the art of intimidation. Now, he licked his lips and desperately hoped he was reading it right when Serihk's gaze darted to his mouth and more purple slowly overtook the green.

"You said I should come back to you if I ever…wanted anything again?"

"I did." Serihk's dark eyes glinted. "That door is still open."

This was it. Bryant swallowed and tried to keep his voice confident. He tried to pretend he was making a tempting proposition and not begging for help. "I'd like to make a deal with you."

Serihk's face shuttered, and Bryant's stomach plummeted.

"And what do you have in mind?" Serihk asked in a flat tone. The patterns of color pulled back off his face and faded. The blank stare Serihk fixed him with made Bryant want to be sick, but he forged ahead. He didn't have any other options.

"I want to leave with you today," he said, stepping closer and dropping his voice. He felt ridiculous trying to put on a sultry tone and make his eyes do that come-hither thing pretty men and women had done to him. But he tried his goddamn best. "To spend all that week back to Qesha *revisiting* this morning's experience."

Serihk's pretty upper lip curled, and he clasped his hands behind his back. All traces of color and pattern drained from his pale skin, and he straightened to his full height. Bryant easily outweighed the qesh, but Serihk was much taller, and the way he looked down on Bryant made him feel very small.

"And is that your offer or your compensation?"

Bryant winced at his tone. "My offer. I need something else."

"And what is that?"

If this had ever been a seduction, it had tipped over

into a plea now, so Bryant dropped the pretense and set his jaw. "I need to get my thirteen-year-old daughter out of here."

Serihk's haughty expression didn't change, it just froze. "What?"

"My thirteen-year-old daughter was set up by a crime boss so he could force me to keep working for him. Now she's due to be transported without trial to a penal colony in an hour." Bryant's legs shook with the instinct to throw himself at this man's feet. "I *need* that to not happen. *Please.*"

Bryant didn't need to be good at reading people to recognize the open revulsion on Serihk's face or even the sudden swirl of black that bloomed up from behind his collar. "And so you'd pay for my help with your body?"

Bryant tried not to feel the sting of seeing disgust in those black eyes that had held interest just a few moments ago. He gritted his teeth. It didn't matter. "Yes."

Emissary Serihk shook his head slowly. Then he scoffed, short and sharp. "No deal."

Bryant opened his mouth, but Serihk didn't give him another chance. He pushed past him, opened the door, and slammed it shut behind him.

Bryant stared at that closed door. Despairing fear overwhelmed him. Fear he hadn't felt since he was nine years old, standing in a hovel in the refugee camp in Carta, watching his mother's body being carted away, and realizing he was all alone.

## Chapter Three

SERIHK STOOD in the hall with rage, embarrassment, and shame boiling up from his chest and threatening to show on his face. He exhaled, smoothed his expression into something less vulnerable, and forced his skin clear.

"That not go how you expected?" Lar'a spared him a glance to raise a horned eyebrow before returning her watchful gaze to the hallway.

That about summed up Serihk's entire morning. He hadn't expected to catch a thief in his ship, and he hadn't expected the thief to be handsome. He hadn't expected his breath to be knocked out of him by the sight of the big man with tears gathering in his eyes, and he certainly hadn't expected the sudden protective fire it had filled him with, or that he would start trying to comfort the man instead of calling the authorities.

He supposed he should have expected his base instincts to take over once the man started making all those little moans and gasps and sighs.

He clenched his teeth. "No. It did not," he replied.

"What happened?"

Serihk thought back to the room behind him, and of Bryant Harrison stepping into his space, still smelling of cum and sex. He thought of the shy smile he'd given him and the way he'd licked his lips. Serihk thought of the way his own heart had jumped and his mouth had watered... until Bryant's façade had cracked, and Serihk had realized that the nervousness in the man's eyes was borne of desperation, not eagerness.

Just like this morning in the ship. All his moans, his frantic nods, his twitching hips... He hadn't wanted it at all. He'd just wanted Serihk to think he did. He'd given Serihk what he thought he wanted because it was the only escape he saw.

Serihk's stomach knotted with nausea. The man was in a terrible position. Terrible enough to offer unfettered access to himself for almost a week to a stranger who had bound him up, impaled him on flex metal tentacles, and watched as he'd writhed and came. And Serihk—greedy, selfish monster that he was—almost wanted to take him up on that offer. Greedy, selfish, and self-delusional because he had been so sure that Bryant had *enjoyed* what they had done—what *Serihk* had done.

Serihk stood straight and frowned hard against the torrent of unpleasantness. There wasn't time to deal with his own hurt feelings right now. "I'll tell you later. There's something I need to do."

He turned to see the station captain striding down the hallway—carrying the ridiculous candelabra Serihk had given Bryant in some absurd attempt at courtship—and started down the hall to meet him.

Serihk had a thirteen-year-old girl and her desperate father to get out of jail.

The negotiation took far less than an hour. The authorities had nothing concrete on which to keep Bryant

Harrison once Serihk confirmed the candelabra had been a gift. They did make multiple references to Bryant's numerous alleged crimes, but that didn't sway Serihk either. Serihk didn't doubt Bryant's guilt given Bryant's own admission to working for a crime boss and that Serihk himself had caught him breaking, entering, and stealing, but he couldn't seem to make himself care. Perhaps it was the foolish infatuation flickering in his chest, but his gut couldn't be convinced that Bryant was a villain either.

Securing Astrid Harrison's freedom was even easier. Serihk didn't have to press hard for it to become clear that her arrest stank of collusion and corruption and that the station didn't want word of that to be spread around. She was also a child, and no one *really* wanted to send her off to hard labor on a desolate moon.

And so it was that Serihk left the pitiful police station in the back of an intra-station transport with one fuming bodyguard beside him and two very confused criminals across from him. Serihk could feel Lar'a's displeasure rolling off her in one constant wave, even though she hadn't dared voice an objection while in the company of others. Bryant was clearly disconcerted and wary, but he stayed silent. Astrid seemed less wary but wore the same stoic expression as her father. They even had the same furrow between their brows.

"Our ship leaves tonight," Serihk said in his most professional voice. "The cooking staff is ensuring we'll have human-appropriate fare, but the servants will need to know where to retrieve your belongings."

Astrid shot a look at her father, and Bryant met her eyes and then looked back at Serihk. "I'll need to take them there myself."

"No official address then?" Lar'a asked in an almost

accusatory tone, and it was Serihk's turn to shoot a look at his companion.

Bryant met her gaze steadily, but his face tightened. Relations between humans and klah'eel were still strained from the war. They were further strained between klah'eel and the humans who had fled as refugees when the Klah'Eel invaded Tava. From what Serihk had gathered at the station, that would have included Bryant.

But Bryant replied in an even tone. "No."

Lar'a nodded and didn't press the issue.

"When we arrive, a servant will show you to your rooms and will then take you wherever you need to go," Serihk continued. "I have business to conclude and will join you later."

Neither Bryant nor Astrid said anything, but they both watched him with matching intense stares, so Serihk went on.

"Bryant, you are familiar with my security system"—he tried to ignore the sudden blush along Bryant's cheeks— "but Astrid, you may not be." Serihk tapped his own temple. "I am neurally linked to my ship and all of its sensors. It has also been fitted with a comprehensive flex metal network."

Astrid swallowed.

"I don't tell you this to threaten or scare you. I promise not to ever hurt or touch you." He met Bryant's eyes to make sure he understood what Serihk was saying. He wouldn't do to Astrid, what he had done to Bryant. Bryant gave him a long look, and then nodded slightly, and Serihk turned back to Astrid. "I merely want to inform you that you should have no expectation of complete privacy while you're aboard, but that you *do* have an expectation of complete security."

He glanced at Bryant again and was surprised to see a

wisp of something vulnerable in his eyes, and Serihk held his gaze as he finished. "My ship is the safest place you could possibly be."

Bryant looked away from him and down at his daughter. Astrid glanced up at him, then back at Serihk. She nodded her understanding, and they finished the rest of the ride in silence.

Serihk didn't interact with his guests again that night. It was late by the time he returned from the station's Klah'Eel embassy. The informal negotiations had gone long and virtually nowhere. Humans were agitating for an interspecies solution to the refugee crisis triggered by the Klah'Eel takeover of Tava. Serihk had brokered the peace deal that had resulted in the Humans ceding the planet, and so they had come to him to clean up the fallout. Humans, at their worst, were governmentally incompetent and incapable of providing the barest of necessities for their people. The Klah'Eel at their worst were cold and uncompromising and believed all humans from Tava should become loyal Klah'Eel citizens. Lately, they were both determined to be at their worst.

When he finally dragged himself back aboard his ship, and they could depart for Qesha, he was in no mood for confused and confusing guests. And yet, his awareness still strayed through the ship's sensors to Bryant, alone in his room. The human sat on the edge of the bed with his bearded chin in his hands and a dark frown furrowing his brows. Every once in a while, he would inhale deeply and let out a long sigh.

Despite the hour, Serihk tried to get some work done. He wanted to make as much progress on his refugee proposals as possible before returning to the Senate. He would only have a couple of weeks in Qesha to meet with them before he had to be in Tava itself. An extremely powerful human family was to discuss investments in Tava's Southern Hemisphere, where most of the remaining humans still lived. If there was any group of humans Serihk trusted less than the Human government itself, it was their collection of oligarchic families.

For Serihk to undermine whatever schemes the Turner family had for Tava, he needed to have his own proposals. And to craft his own proposals, he needed information. And so he read reports. Reports, and reports, and reports and studies from organizations that ranged from explicitly biased to implicitly biased. Human and civil rights groups, Klah'Eel citizens groups, refugee aid organizations, war counsels, the Klah-Eel and Human governments themselves, the various planetary and station governments that were most acutely feeling the strain of the sudden refugee influx, and on and on and on.

Periodically, Serihk's attention would stray back to Bryant, sitting on the bed, deep in thought. Serihk wondered what *he* would think of the Klah'Eel's claim that the refugees would be better off if they returned and renounced their loyalty to the Human species state, or of the planetary government of Carta's claim that all refugees were violent and lawless criminals that should be effectively barred from society.

Eventually, after setting aside another shallow report with an agenda, Serihk sat back and rubbed his eyes. His bedroom was beckoning, and his chair—as exquisite as it was—was making his back sore. Everyone else had long since fallen asleep: Lar'a in her quarters next to his, the few servants in the starboard wing, and Astrid, curled up in the center of the bed in her guest room.

Everyone but Bryant, who had lain in bed by now and pulled the covers up to his chin but still stared at the ceiling. Serihk watched him for a moment and then sent a message to the cook's tablet to make something delightful for the humans for breakfast.

The next morning, smells of something spiced and rich wafted down the hall to him as Serihk walked to the dining room. He heard a girl's quick laughter as he approached and then a deep answering guffaw, and something warm bloomed in his chest.

When he entered the room, Astrid and Bryant were smiling broadly at each other with matching crooked grins. But their expressions dropped into seriousness when they saw Serihk, and the little warm thing in his chest extinguished. He forced himself to give them a smile, but he knew it came out more official than intimate and immediately felt more awkward.

"Good morning. I hope you slept well." He sat down across the table from them and reached for his usual fruit. In front of the humans sat a large platter of buns, slathered with white frosting and so sticky they sat on the plate as a unit with pieces torn off. Astrid's plate had the remains of one. Bryant's still had half of one. And their fingers were covered with frosting.

"Yes, thank you," Astrid replied. And Serihk tried not to show his surprise. She'd been silent in the car, and he'd been worried she'd stay that way.

"Very well, thank you," Bryant said.

Serihk knew that was a lie, but he let it go. He wondered if Bryant remembered or realized that Serihk could be watching him. Then Bryant brought his frosting-covered thumb up to his mouth and slipped it between his lips, and Serihk lost the capacity to wonder about anything.

Their eyes caught, and the human froze. Serihk was sure that licking one's fingers was quite a normal thing to do. The frosting was undoubtedly delicious. The buns were clearly sticky and required the use of fingers. Astrid was licking hers right next to him. But the sight of Bryant's pursed lips and hollowed cheeks made Serihk swallow hard.

Bryant's eyes widened and darted to Serihk's throat, where Serihk knew traitorous purple swirls were eddying on his skin. Then Bryant looked away and wiped the rest of his fingers off on his napkin.

A few moments later, Lar'a walked in and saved Serihk's stuttering brain from trying to think of what to say next. She glanced at him with narrowed eyes and then at Bryant, her nose twitching.

"Good morning." Her loud voice boomed in the awkwardly silent room. She set her training staff in the corner and sat next to Serihk, throwing him one more suspicious look. Then she smiled at Astrid and Bryant. She and Serihk hadn't had a chance to discuss Serihk's snap decision on taking in guests, but she at least seemed to have decided not to take it out on them. Serihk hoped they'd had enough positive interactions with klah'eel to recognize the sharp teeth and tusk-filled expression as friendly. She pointed at the plate of buns. "Those smell delicious. Can I have one?"

"Sure," Astrid chirped with surprising enthusiasm. "They're really good. They're cinnamon rolls."

"I've never had a cinnamon roll," Lar'a said, ripping one off.

"Me neither, but I see them in the nicer part of the station sometimes."

Bryant's deep voice surprised Serihk when he addressed him. "Do you want one?"

Serihk flicked his eyes down to the platter. They looked very messy and very sweet. And he never varied his breakfast. He cut himself off another piece of his fruit. "No, thank you."

Bryant just nodded, and Serihk had the disappointing feeling he'd somehow missed an opportunity for something.

"Do you fight with that?" Astrid pointed to Lar'a's staff in the corner, and Lar'a scoffed.

"No, I just train with that," she said. "My real gatlung is much more impressive."

She and Astrid launched into a conversation about Lar'a's favorite topic—tools of violence. Not that Serihk judged her for it. Her love for tools of violence had been keeping him safe for years.

Neither Serihk nor Bryant interjected, letting Lar'a hold forth while Astrid peppered her with questions. Serihk ate his fruit slowly, and drank his klak, and Bryant ate two more buns. His shoulders still looked tense, but nerves at least didn't dull his appetite. Or maybe he was just good at eating when food was available regardless.

They met each other's eyes occasionally, but Bryant always looked away again before Serihk could give him even a brief smile.

"Can I, Dad?" Astrid looked at Bryant, already halfway off her seat.

"What?" Bryant clearly hadn't been following the conversation any more closely than Serihk had.

"Can I go see Lar'a's armory?"

"Oh. Sure."

Astrid hopped all the way off her seat, Lar'a grabbed one of the last buns, and they left Serihk and Bryant to sit alone at the table together. Once the sound of their voices had faded away, Bryant sat back in his chair and wiped his hands clean. Serihk set aside his utensils, laced his fingers together, and rested his hands in front of him.

"Have you changed your mind then?" Bryant asked after a beat. He tossed his napkin back onto the table, crossed his arms, and met Serihk's gaze with a set but not grim expression.

"About what?"

"Our deal."

"No."

Bryant's eyes narrowed. "Then what are you doing?"

"I like to think I'm helping," Serihk replied, and that must have been the wrong thing to say because the crease between Bryant's brows deepened.

"Out of what, the goodness of your heart?"

"You make that sound like a bad thing."

"You normally spring human refugees from jail and fly them to the other side of the system?" Bryant raised an eyebrow, and Serihk pressed his lips together.

"I'm not interested in taking your body as payment for your daughter's life." It galled Serihk that he could be read as someone that *would* be interested. And it galled him all the more that he couldn't think of a single reason anyone would consider him any kinder. He had a professional reputation as a cold and unfeeling bastard, and he didn't have any personal relations that would dispute it either. And maybe they were all right because a small—*tiny*—part of him still wanted to take the deal if it was the only way he could get his hands on this man.

"I've given a lot more for a lot less," Bryant said, and the tiny part of Serihk that wanted to take the deal shriveled up and died. The thought of his touch being merely tolerated made him nauseated and left him feeling small and pathetic.

He scowled. "I don't know if you think that's flattering, but it's not."

Bryant didn't reply, but he at least had the grace to

grimace and look away. They lapsed into a tense silence. Serihk felt like there was something more to say, but for the life of him, he couldn't think of what it was. He went into diplomatic talks with a goal and an agenda, but he wasn't at all sure what he wanted here.

He cocked his attention to Lar'a and Astrid, and a smile twitched his lips.

"You should know that Lar'a is about to give Astrid an intro lesson on using gatlungs."

Bryant huffed a laugh. "That's fine. Probably good for her."

Serihk nodded and stood. Solving the refugee crisis and Southern Tava's descent into poverty suddenly seemed quite feasible compared to navigating whatever this was.

"I really don't owe you anything for this?" Bryant asked before Serihk left.

Serihk turned to look back at Bryant, and his heart twisted in his chest. He smiled softly at the big man, hoping that conveyed at least something.

"You really don't."

Bryant nodded. But if Serihk had managed to convey something, it hadn't been comfort. Bryant's brow furrowed, his face darkened, and he looked away. So Serihk left, feeling even worse than when he'd walked in.

---

"SO, Astrid is worried some sort of system-wide gang is going to hunt down her and her father after we get back to Qesha," Lar'a announced without preamble. She strode into Serihk's study, still sweaty from her workout, and dropped down in the leather armchair Serihk often used for diplomatic guests.

"I'm sure she is." Serihk set down his tablet. "Is that why she asked you how to use your gatlung?"

"I think it was one reason. Is that why you brought them on board?"

"More or less."

"Her dad's a jumpy one. He stinks of fear, even sitting at the breakfast table."

"I think he has good reason given his upbringing."

"Probably."

"You seem more kindly disposed to him than you were yesterday," Serihk said.

Lar'a shrugged. "I did the math. He was too young when we took Tava to have left on his own. His shitty situation is more his parents' fault than his."

"How generous of you," Serihk said dryly. Lar'a was of the opinion that all the humans on Tava should have stayed when the Klah-Eel invaded and integrated into Klah-Eel society. She had minimal sympathy for the ones that had fled and cared barely at all for their current predicaments. "Do you need something, Lar'a?"

"I checked the security system. He got in with door codes. The ones we gave to the Qeshian embassy so they could drop off all those treaty hard copies. I told them they have a leak."

"Very good."

Lar'a didn't get up to leave, though, so Serihk sighed. "Something else?"

"Yeah. You gonna tell me why you gave him that gaudy monstrosity in the first place?" Lar'a asked. Serihk thought the candelabra was actually rather elegant, but he wouldn't win that argument.

"Do you need to know?" he asked instead. Lar'a would have smelled the cum on Bryant the day before, and she would have smelled Serihk's arousal at least a few times at breakfast. But he really didn't want to go into detail about how he had a strange compulsion to shower lovers in luxury after getting them off. Calling Bryant a lover would have stretched the truth to the point of snapping anyway.

"Did you want him to get caught?"

Serihk reared back. "What? No. I'd already caught him."

"Then why did you give him something so hard to move?" Lar'a scrunched up her face, and Serihk's stomach sank.

"I had just meant to give him something nice," he admitted. "It didn't occur to me that there was a practical upper limit on his side."

"Shocker." Lar'a sighed and stood back up. "Well, worked out for him anyway, I guess."

"What?" Serihk raised his eyebrows. "No scolding about rash and impulsive decisions?"

Lar'a shrugged and waved a hand as she left. "You're projecting. Those bother you, not me."

Serihk scowled and went back to his work, irritated with himself and his numerous miscalculations.

Serihk took dinner at his desk, partly because they were days from reaching Qesha and he had work to do, and partly to save the dinner conversation from the weight of his presence. He watched them, though. Or rather, if he were honest, he watched Bryant. Astrid chattered at him nonstop, explaining to him all Lar'a had taught her that day, with occasional clarifying interjections from Lar'a herself. He indulged her with questions and exclamations at all the appropriate times.

Serihk knew little of human parent-child relationships, but Bryant's expressions and the way he clapped her shoulder all spoke of affection beyond what Serihk had ever expected of his own father. The warm smile Bryant wore as he watched his daughter engage with Lar'a was breathtaking, and it made Serihk's belly churn with a frustrated longing that turned his food to dust in his mouth.

After they finished up, Lar'a showed them to the library and revealed to Astrid the clutch of adventure books from Serihk's childhood that he kept on a bottom shelf hidden behind a chair. As a boy, he'd admired the gallant heroes. As he grew older and more jaded, he'd realized the villains were usually more efficient with their time and energy.

"Wait, Astrid," Bryant started before she could grab one—and she'd been heading for an excellent choice. Bryant looked at Lar'a. "Will he be upset?"

"He can see us, remember?" Lar'a twirled a finger over her head to encompass all the tiny sensors Serihk was indeed watching them through. "If he didn't want us to, he'd stop us. Besides, assuming she doesn't rip it to shreds, he'll like that they're being read."

That was a touch more sentimental than Serihk actually felt about his books, but it was true that Astrid was welcome to them.

Bryant did not seem to have remembered that Serihk could be—and in this case was—watching them, and he crossed his arms with a guarded expression. But he let Astrid make her selection. And when she trotted off back to her room to read, he caught Lar'a's attention.

"Thank you." He nodded to the doorway Astrid had disappeared through. "For—"

Lar'a tsked and waved her big hand. "It's nothing. Have a good night."

Serihk rolled his eyes; Lar'a had never been good at accepting thanks.

After she left, Bryant stayed in the library. He stood there for a few minutes, looking around at the full shelves, arms still crossed and fingertips white from where they dug into his biceps. Eventually, he sat down at the table, pulled out his two-generation-old tablet, and started pouring over it with his forehead propped on his left hand and his fingers curled in his hair. He looked as frustrated with whatever he was working on as Serihk was.

So Serihk left them both to it, bringing his attention back to the report on refugee educational attainment that he'd mentally abandoned for the actual refugee on his ship. A couple of hours later, Serihk's eyes were crossing, and Bryant still sat at the table alone in the library. So, Serihk did what he'd wanted to do all day.

Bryant looked up with a flicker of surprise as Serihk entered the room and cleared the tablet's screen with a quick swipe.

"Do you need this room?" he asked, moving to stand from his chair.

Serihk waved him back down. "Not at all. I wanted to join you, if I may?"

"Oh." Bryant didn't go for the door, but he didn't sit back down either. "Sure."

"Would you like a drink?" Serihk moved to the decanter set on the small table next to his shelf of legal books. The books were for show more than anything else—if he actually needed to know something, he'd call it to his tablet—but he did like looking at them.

"Sure," Bryant said again, and Serihk heard a tiny, frustrated sound. "I mean, yes, please."

Serihk poured them two glasses of the deep purple liquid. It was a Qeshian drink, but he'd recently served it to a human official who had approved. He carried them both to the deep armchairs in the corner, and Bryant followed him. He passed one to Bryant, and they each sank into one of the chairs. The human took a sip, gave the beverage a surprised look, and then took a larger swallow. Bryant looked good like that, sitting in a luxurious chair and drinking a luxurious vintage from a crystal glass. Serihk felt that urge again to give him all the nice things he could think of.

"I wanted to apologize," Serihk said after a few moments of almost comfortable silence.

Bryant snorted and glanced around pointedly. "For what?"

"For the candelabra." Serihk sighed. He didn't enjoy owning up to such a foolish mistake, but he'd rather admit he was a fool than have Bryant think he was a snake. If it had occurred to Lar'a that Serihk might have gotten Bryant caught on purpose, it could have occurred to Bryant. "I didn't mean to give you something that would get you in trouble. I don't have a great understanding of criminal dealings."

"I figured." Bryant chuckled. After a beat, he worried his lower lip, as though debating with himself, and then asked, "Why did you give it to me?"

"It's nicer than the dagger, and I thought nicer was strictly better."

"But why give me anything at all? I was stealing from you." Bryant grimaced. "Was it payment? For what I let you do to me?"

Serihk felt like Bryant had punched him in the gut. *What he'd let Serihk do to him.* That was the crux of the problem, wasn't it? Serihk had taken something he shouldn't have. He had thought the pleasure was mutual. He'd been so delusional he'd felt like he had been *caring* for the man who had been so clearly burdened under so much weight. He'd thought the way Bryant's muscles had gone pliant under his flex metal had been from a welcomed relief. What was wrong with him? He inhaled shakily and carefully set his glass on the table beside him, but Bryant spoke before he did.

"Fuck, I'm sorry." Bryant stood quickly and walked a few paces away. He scrubbed his hand over his face. "I shouldn't have asked that. I know it wasn't."

"It really wasn't." Serihk stood too, looking at Bryant's back. "But what I did—"

"I liked it." Bryant shot him a firm look over his shoulder. "I liked it, and I wanted it. So whatever you're going to say, don't."

Bryant kept their gazes locked until Serihk managed a nod. He kept his face smooth, but his mind raced, and he could only imagine what colors and patterns were swarming over his skin. Bryant *had* liked it. Serihk had been so sure at the time, but his certainty had crumbled the moment Bryant had tried to make that deal. He had been so worried that Bryant had seen him as a man that took advantage because that was what he had done.

But Bryant had liked it, had wanted it even, which meant maybe he might want it again. Serihk stepped closer and opened his mouth but didn't get a word out before the door opened.

"Dad! I—Oh." Astrid stopped short and stood stock-still in the doorway, eyes flicking between Serihk and Bryant.

Serihk shoved all his feelings back down and tried to clear his skin. He inclined his head to the girl. "Good evening, Astrid."

"I'm sorry." She shuffled her feet. "I just wanted to talk to my dad."

"Later, Astrid," Bryant said with a huskiness in his voice that hadn't been there a moment ago, but Serihk shook his head.

"No, it's fine. I should be getting to bed." He drained

his glass and set it on a table for a servant to clean up in the morning. If he stayed alone in that room with Bryant any longer, he'd either jump him or beg him. He wasn't at all sure Bryant would be receptive to either, and he'd rather he didn't make a fool of himself. "Goodnight to you both."

Bryant looked like he was going to say something, but then he closed his mouth and nodded.

Serihk returned to his room and readied for bed, trying and mostly failing to keep his awareness off Bryant. Astrid had had a nightmare, which she wasn't so concerned about, but she *was* concerned about the real-life people she had been dreaming of: the criminal gang they had so far managed to escape.

She wanted to know what they were going to do when they got to Qesha and how they would disappear. Bryant told her he was working on it and motioned to his tablet still on the table. He told her he wasn't worried and that they would be fine. He said it so confidently that even Serihk was convinced until Bryant wrapped Astrid in a hug, set his chin on the top of her head, and let his face crumple. For just a moment, his strong features fell into a look of such dread and despair that Serihk's heart stopped. But then Bryant rearranged them into something soft and sure and leaned back to look down into Astrid's face with a small smile.

Astrid went back to bed, looking comforted, and Bryant stood alone in the library again. He dragged a hand over his face, then swallowed the rest of his drink and set his glass down next to Serihk's. Serihk lay in bed, wrapped in his covers, and watched Bryant return to his room and climb into his own bed. He watched Bryant as he tossed and turned, wondering how he could help him, until he drifted off to sleep.

Serihk had aligned his awareness with Bryant so tightly that when Bryant awoke with a strangled scream, Serihk sat bolt upright with a gasp. He focused on Bryant. The man was sitting on the opulent bed, hunched over with his hands fisted in the sheets. His head hung, and his shoulders shuddered.

Serihk's heart clenched. He felt the same strange, protective urge he'd felt when he'd found him in the ship holding back tears. It was that urge to hold back everything that could be wrong and to take the man somewhere soft and safe. He unfolded a small tendril from the molding under Bryant's bed and reached up to brush away the single tear that had gathered at the corner of his eye. Bryant jerked away but then saw the tentacle and sighed.

"I guess it was too much to hope you'd be asleep," he said, and Serihk smiled ruefully to himself. Things would be a lot easier for him too, if he'd just slept through this. Now, his mind was racing with how to make all of this man's problems disappear, and his chest was filled with an overwhelming urge to hold him.

Then Bryant closed his eyes and leaned back toward the tentacle. Serihk's stomach swooped, and he quickly soothed the flex metal over the man's cheek. He stroked Bryant's face and watched some of the tightness around his eyes bleed away. He unfolded more tentacles from the wall and brushed them into Bryant's hair. Serihk remembered he had liked that before, and sure enough, Bryant's breath caught, and then he let out a little groan and went boneless against the headboard.

Serihk sat up in his own bed, feet on the ground, blind to his own surroundings. He was too caught up in what he could see and hear and feel through the ship in Bryant's room. He watched Bryant's eyes flutter closed, listened to his breath quicken, and felt the heat of his sleep-warmed skin. Serihk moved his massage down to Bryant's neck, and Bryant bit his lip and shifted his hips. Serihk glanced down from his face and saw the outline of his half-hard cock through his thin sleeping pants. Serihk groaned and was thankful for the hallway of distance that would cover the sound.

"Will you...?" Bryant whispered. He squeezed his eyes shut and then opened them again and spoke to the empty room. "Will you fuck me again? Please?"

"Oh goddess, yes," Serihk groaned, and his cock throbbed. But Bryant couldn't hear him, so he answered with a fresh cluster of tentacles flowing over the bed. They wrapped around Bryant's ankles and wrists and secured them to the mattress.

Bryant moaned lightly, his muscles releasing and his cock stiffening enough to tent his pants. Serihk licked his lips. He pulled Bryant down until he lay flat on the bed, wrists locked up above him against the headboard.

Serihk paused to catch his breath. Bryant liked this, *wanted* this, *wanted* Serihk to be in total control. He trusted him. That was overwhelming and energizing, and Serihk had to stand out of bed and pace across the room to consider his next move and to rein his own lust back in. He wanted to be sweet. He wanted this to be all about comfort and care and to make Bryant boneless and sated and to watch him fall into a deep and luxurious sleep afterward. Serihk couldn't refrain from palming himself, the sudden arousal overwhelming. He gave his own rock-hard length a few strokes before he focused back in on Bryant.

Bryant stretched out on the bed, his muscles pliant and his cock hard. There was already a spot of dampness at its head.

Serihk brushed a tentacle along Bryant's cheek and trailed it down his neck. He dragged it over his collarbones and into the dark of his shirt. He circled his right nipple a few times, then plucked at it to hear the way it made Bryant's breath catch and made him squirm. Then he snaked over the man's abs, which clenched and twitched. When he got to the hem of Bryant's shirt, he wrapped around it and pulled it back over his head. Then he eased the waistbands of his pants and underwear over his cock and tossed them to the side. He needed to see what he was working with, and being stripped bare drew out another little moan from Bryant.

Serihk was immediately drawn to the man's pulsing balls, and his mouth watered. He wrapped a few tendrils around them, feeling the heft of them, the soft skin of the sack. He pulled them gently away from Bryant's body and saw the man's thighs twitch.

So he swarmed tentacles over them, rolled and fondled them and watched Bryant tremble with the stimulation. Serihk drank in the way his face contorted and the way he licked his lips and bit off his moans. He was so beautiful. Serihk cupped his jaw with flex metal and stroked over his cheekbone. Bryant turned into the caress, and Serihk reached farther with his tentacles to cradle the back of the man's head, to hold him as he played with his balls.

What Serihk wouldn't give to kiss him, to have his hands on his hard body. He wished he could feel the way his muscles clenched and shuddered while Serihk played with him. He wished he could really see his desperate expression instead of this shallow stream from the ship's sensors.

"Oh fuck, Serihk…" Bryant whined as he arched his back and pulled on his bound wrists.

The sound of his name on Bryant's lips almost brought Serihk to his knees. Goddess, he wished he could be in the room with him. He tightened the tentacles around Bryant's ankles and stretched him longer on the bed, and Bryant let his muscles go slack with a sigh.

Once Bryant's breathy moans turned to whimpers, Serihk finally wrapped a warm tentacle around his leaking cock. He went slow and gentle. Slow and gentle and inexorable. Bryant would come on Serihk's time, but he would come. Serihk would make sure he got what he wanted, and Bryant would take it from him.

Bryant gritted his teeth and twitched his hips up into the too-loose grasp. His cockhead was near purple now. "Please," he breathed.

Serihk brushed a lock of hair away from his face but didn't speed up. Bryant twisted and raked his teeth over his lip but then visibly forced himself back down. He nosed at the tentacles cradling his head, and Serihk petted him more, comforted him as he brought him torturously close to the edge.

Bryant gave in to Serihk. He handed him all the power and all the control. He trusted him to take care of him even while it felt overwhelming. The thought made Serihk's balls tighten, and he breathed through the thrill of arousal. This man would ruin him. Maybe he already had.

After endless more moments, Bryant sobbed.

"Please," he begged again, and Serihk took pity this time.

He tightened the grip he had on his cock and slid another tentacle between his legs. He sped up his pulls as he stroked firmly against the spot behind Bryant's lovely balls, and Bryant came with a cry.

He strained against Serihk's metal, bulky muscles standing out in stark relief. Cum shot from the tip of his cock and up his belly and chest in spurts and pulses. Then he fell limp, shaking with aftershocks. Serihk slowly unwound his tentacles from around the man's wrists and ankles. There were red lines from where he had pulled against them, but judging by the blissed-out expression on Bryant's face, he didn't seem to mind.

Serihk grabbed a far corner of the huge sheet that covered the bed and wiped the cum off Bryant's chest and stomach, then pulled a clean section over the top of him. Bryant opened his eyes blearily and reached out toward the tentacles. He tangled his fingers in them, and Serihk's heart flipped at the strange intimacy of it.

"Thank you," Bryant murmured. Serihk touched his face one last time as his eyes dropped closed, and he pulled all his tentacles back into the wall.

Serihk came back to himself, standing in the center of his room, breathing fast and so hard it hurt. He shoved his robe open and wrapped his hand around his cock. The feel of his hand over his weeping, neglected length had him moaning and his knees buckling.

He rubbed himself frantically, thinking of Bryant's whimpers, his moans, the way he had nuzzled toward Serihk's touch as the stimulation overwhelmed him. He thought of what he would do if he were there. How he would have spread him and taken those exquisitely sensitive balls in his mouth, how he would have tongued—

Serihk seized up and came all over his hand, the imagined taste of Bryant's musk on his tongue. As the aftershocks wore off, he sat down hard on his bed. He had gotten himself in deep. He didn't know into *what* exactly, but he was deep.

He looked again at Bryant, fast asleep in the soft bed Serihk had tucked him into. He smiled despite the nervous flutter in his stomach and the looming sense of dread somewhere deeper inside of him.

## Chapter Four

THE NEXT MORNING, Serihk arrived at breakfast before the humans and had a choice to make. He could take some klak and fruit back to his study and hide away, or he could stay and make small talk with Bryant and pretend he hadn't just put his ship's security system all over his body and then gotten off to the thought. He chose to sit.

He had just finished pouring his klak when Bryant and Astrid arrived.

"Good morning, sir," Astrid chirped.

"Good morning." He nodded to them. "I hope you both had good nights."

Bryant's cheeks turned pink, but Astrid spoke before he opened his mouth.

"I did. You have the softest blankets I've ever used," she said, piling scrambled chicken's eggs and toast onto her plate. "And the best food."

Serihk laughed. "I'm glad you like them."

"And thank you for letting me borrow your book. I'm almost done with it already."

"You picked a good one. You should hurry with it. The second one's even better."

Astrid's eyes lit up as she grinned. "Okay!" Then she shoveled food into her mouth.

Serihk smiled at Bryant over his glass, and Bryant looked away from his happy daughter to smile back at him.

"And how did you sleep?" he asked Serihk, raising an eyebrow.

Serihk smirked. "Particularly well," he said in a low voice and was gratified to see the pink on Bryant's cheeks darken.

They ate in silence, Astrid wolfing down her food twice if not three times as fast. "Lar'a said I should meet her in the gym as soon as I'm done. And I overslept, so I'm gonna go there now."

"Don't throw up," Bryant said as Astrid slid off her chair.

"I won't." Astrid didn't roll her eyes, but her tone did. "See you later."

Serihk chucked as she left, and Bryant sighed. "Thank you," he said when she was gone.

Serihk cocked his head. "For what?"

"For indulging her so much," he said. "She's been enjoying this."

"Good." Serihk nodded. "I'm sure she deserves it after what she went through back on the station."

Bryant's mouth twisted humorlessly, and he looked down at his coffee cup. "And everything else in her life."

"She's worried about what happens when we get to Qesha," Serihk said, carefully setting his cup back on its saucer and tapping his forefinger against the rim.

"Yeah." Bryant nodded.

"So are you."

"Yeah." Bryant nodded again and then looked back up at Serihk. "Can we not talk about it, please?"

"Of course." Serihk frowned. "My apologies."

"No, it's just—" Bryant shook his head. "I'd rather not right now."

"Sure."

They lapsed into silence, and Serihk's heart slowly sank.

He was about to get up when Bryant spoke again. "So." He drew out the syllable and shrugged awkwardly. "What are you doing when you're holed up in your study?"

Serihk recognized the clumsy attempt at small talk and his heart lifted again.

"Trying to make highly impactful and yet barely informed decisions mostly," he replied, wrinkling his nose. "A lot of reading reports by people who don't know what they're talking about or don't care, so I can recommend a course of action, the results of which will never directly affect me."

Bryant raised his brows.

"And that's if I'm lucky," Serihk continued. "If I'm unlucky, I spend a lot of time trying to foil the plans of selfish bad actors like the Turner family."

"I've heard of them." Bryant nodded. "They're saying they're going to bring thousands of jobs to Southern Tava."

"Yes, I'm sure they are." Serihk lifted his mug to his lips. "Saying that, I mean."

"I know a lot of humans who are thinking about moving back because of it," Bryant said. "Life on Carta and Lewis Station hasn't exactly worked out well for a lot of us."

"No, I've gathered that," Serihk said. "I'm just not

convinced the Turner family is the right answer. But I understand they're a tempting one."

Serihk looked down at his empty place and cocked his head as a thought came to him.

"What?"

"Hm?" Serihk looked back up at Bryant to see the human watching him with narrowed eyes.

"What are you thinking?"

Serihk smiled. "I'm thinking you could help me."

Bryant burst out a bark of laughter. He shook his head. "You need someone beat up or scared straight?"

Serihk shook his head. "No. And if I did, I'm sure Lar'a could handle that."

"Probably better than me," Bryant admitted, and he didn't look in the least ashamed of it, still grinning at Serihk.

"I need a consultant."

Bryant's jovial expression fell. He shifted in his seat and crossed his arms over his chest. "I don't think I'm exactly qualified for that."

"You are, though." Serihk leaned forward, becoming surer of his idea. "I'm working with the Klah'Eel and Human governments to deal with the refugees from Tava. How to house them, feed them, employ them."

"Alright." Bryant's expression stayed guarded.

"Everyone involved in the negotiations are people outside the situation, giving their own opinions and pushing their own agendas," Serihk said. "But this has been your whole life. I could use your insights."

"I don't have any insights into anything." Bryant shook his head. "I just put my head down and try to keep Astrid alive."

"And you have." Serihk reached across the table and put his hand on Bryant's arm and then immediately worried he'd gone too far. "I really do think you could help."

Bryant stared at Serihk's hand on his forearm, and his mouth twisted. Then he sighed and looked back up into Serihk's face. "I'll try. Of course. If it's something you want, then of course I'll try."

Serihk's heart fluttered, and he pulled his hand back with a smile that he had a feeling showed too much. "Thank you."

They drained their coffee and their klak, and Serihk led Bryant back to his study. He wasn't sure where to start, so he began simply pouring information over him. He sat Bryant down at the desk and stacked data tablet after data tablet in front of him. He tried to organize them into piles based on topic, but it turned out not to matter much.

Bryant had a knack for synthesizing information. Serihk had been worried that some of the highly academic and legal language might be too much for him to understand, and maybe it was, but that didn't stop him. He'd frown down at it until he could pull out the pieces of information that told him something. If that didn't work, he'd pass it off to Serihk and ask him to summarize the main points for him, and then he'd move on to the next thing.

He'd poke holes in the findings with offhand comments that Serihk would have to stop him to explain. Like how arrests in the camps on the Human planets closest to Tava weren't lower because there was lower crime, but because the police forces were on the take. Or how the refugee outflow hadn't slowed from Carta, the smuggling operations had just become more sophisticated—that was how he and Astrid had gotten out. And how many people turned to crime instead of factories for employment because the pay was better and they were less likely to be laid off by the local crime syndicates than by the corporations.

With each passing hour, Serihk felt more and more capable of getting a mental handle on the situation. Resolving it would be a thorny, years-long affair, but he could at least begin to understand it now.

And with each passing hour, another layer of tension and armor rolled off Bryant. He sat comfortably at Serihk's desk. He shared his opinions, and he argued against Serihk's. He laughed at Serihk's dry comments, and made some of his own, until they spent as much time laughing as debating.

It was afternoon by the time Serihk's attention was pulled from the office by Astrid on the other side of the ship as she opened the door to Bryant's bedroom with a frown. "I think Astrid is looking for you."

"Hm?" Bryant looked up from the tablet he'd had his crooked nose to and rubbed at his eyes. "Oh. For lunch, probably. I didn't realize it was so late."

"The cook is probably irritated his food is going cold," Serihk said.

Bryant huffed, then stood and stretched. His shoulders popped, and his shirt lifted enough to show off a strip of skin stretched over abdominal muscles and hips that Serihk couldn't force himself to look away from. He was distracted enough to miss whatever Bryant had said, and when Bryant dropped his arms, Serihk blinked back up to his face.

"What was that?"

"I said, we can pick this up again after," Bryant repeated, lifting an eyebrow with a little quirk to his lips that told Serihk he knew exactly what had distracted him. "I want to read that opinion piece by Tava's old governor."

"Sure." Serihk nodded. "We can go all day if you've got the stamina."

"I've got plenty of stamina," Bryant replied, and he gave Serihk a grin that made his mouth water.

The next day, Serihk had an idea. They had spent the rest of the previous day working and finished it with a drink. Then Bryant had joined him back in his study after breakfast, stayed with him for lunch, and by the time he joined him again after that, Serihk had decided it was a perfect idea.

"I'd like to offer you a job," Serihk said once Bryant had finished scribbling down a note.

Bryant frowned. "What kind of job?" he asked after a beat.

"Doing this." Serihk waved his hand to encompass the crowded desk. "An official position as a consultant for my work drafting proposals for the refugee crisis."

Bryant's lips twisted in a way that resembled a smile but definitely wasn't. He leaned back in his chair. "Right," he said. "And what would that look like? Just like this?"

Serihk heard the trap in Bryant's tone, but he didn't know where it was. He straightened his back and laced his fingers together. "It would look similar," he agreed. "You would stay aboard my ship, as would Astrid, obvi—"

"Eating dessert and reading adventure books?"

"If she likes."

Bryant scoffed and crossed his arms.

Serihk carefully kept his face neutral and his skin clear while his insides squirmed. This wasn't going at all how he thought it would. "And I would also pay you a salary," he continued.

"I'm sure you think you're being very kind." Bryant shook his head as he stood up. "But I'm not interested."

Serihk did, in fact, think he was being very kind. He also thought he was being very pragmatic and quite clever.

Serihk rose to stand as well, and even with the desk between them, it accentuated their height difference. "It solves all of your problems."

"Is that what you think?" Bryant scowled and his hands twitched.

"Doesn't it?" Serihk tilted his chin in a way he knew was condescending, but he couldn't stop himself. He was back on the wrong foot, and he was struggling to get himself steady again. Arguing with Bryant was different from arguing with politicians. "It keeps you safe, fed, sheltered, and provides you gainful employment. What else do you need?"

"From you, nothing." Bryant started striding around the desk to the door.

Angry, ugly frustration flared in Serihk. He moved quickly to block Bryant's path. "You're afraid of what happens when we get to Qesha," he snapped. "Astrid is—"

"Don't talk to me about my daughter."

"Then I'll talk about you." Serihk gritted his teeth and stepped closer so that Bryant had to look up at him to keep eye contact. "I didn't spring you from jail so you could wander back out there to be arrested again, or tortured, or killed—"

"No, you sprang me from jail so you could feel like a goddamn hero." Bryant shoved against Serihk's chest and sent him stumbling backward. Flex metal instinctively shot out of the walls and wrapped tightly around both of Bryant's arms. Bryant looked at them and barked out a humorless laugh. "Is it playing the hero that gets you off? You wanna save me as foreplay for fucking me?"

Serihk took a sharp step away from him. A stiff, icy knot of hurt and shame pushed up into his throat, and he tried to swallow around it, but it wouldn't go down. He let his tentacles fall loose, and Bryant wrenched himself free.

"I'm sorry I'm not playing my part," he sneered.

The ugly expression made Serihk flinch. He let Bryant push past him back to the door. Hot frustration had started to melt the ice in his throat, and he wanted to turn around and yell at Bryant, but he clenched his teeth to lock in whatever stupid thing he would have said. He didn't turn around when he heard the door slam, but he watched through the ship's sensors as Bryant stormed down the hall.

Once he was gone, Serihk let out a snarl and slammed his hand on his desk.

He wanted to say that Bryant was wrong. He felt in his *bones* that Bryant was wrong. Serihk wasn't just using Bryant to make himself feel good. Bryant wasn't just a victim to Serihk that he could save to get himself off.

But the feelings that made him want to tie Bryant to a bed and pleasure him until he screamed were all tangled up with the feelings that made him want to ensconce him in blankets and make him laugh until he cried. He couldn't pry them all apart and choose some and leave the others. He couldn't call some the causes and some the effects.

He twisted his hands together and turned away from his desk before he gave into the juvenile impulse to fling everything on it onto the ground.

Dinner was a tense affair that night. Serihk didn't attend, but he watched. Bryant arrived first, as grim-faced as when he'd left Serihk's study. Astrid came in soon after, with a spring in her step that died as soon as she caught sight of her father's face. When Lar'a entered, her nostrils flared, and she quickly filled a plate and left without bothering to feign an excuse.

Astrid nibbled a roll and glanced at her father.

"Tomorrow's our last full day here. We get to Qesha the day after."

"I know."

"I like it here."

"I know."

"I wish we could stay."

Bryant sighed. "That's not realistic, Astrid."

Serihk nearly tore into the room and yelled that it absolutely was realistic if Bryant wasn't such a stubborn bastard, but he managed to dig his fingers into the fabric of his armchair and restrain himself.

"Don't you want to stay?" Astrid demanded.

"It's not that simple," Bryant said evenly, but Astrid threw down her fork.

"I don't want to go back to how it was before," she cried. "I don't *want* to be a criminal. I don't *want* to steal. I don't *want* to live in—"

"And you think I want that for you?" Bryant cut in. "Do you think if I could get you *any* other life, I wouldn't do that?"

"I think you're scared!"

"Of course I'm scared!" Bryant shoved his plate away and spun to face Astrid. He grabbed her upper arm and leaned in close. "And you should be too. Don't get comfortable. You let your guard down for one second, Astrid, and you're dead."

Astrid's lower lip trembled, and her eyes teared up.

Bryant's face didn't soften. "Now go to your room."

He let go of her arm, and she bolted from her chair. She didn't cry until she was out into the hall, and even then, she tried to hold it in, screwing her face up and scrubbing tears from her cheeks. Bryant's stern, almost callous scowl didn't fall until the door closed. Then Serihk saw the brief flash of a devastated expression before Bryant dropped his face into his hands.

No one slept well that night. Serihk lay awake in bed and watched them all toss and turn: Astrid, Bryant, even Lar'a. By the time they were all sitting at the breakfast table, no one had the energy to be at anyone else's throat.

"Are you still going to teach me kato two today, Lar'a?" Astrid asked in a small voice when they were almost done. It was the first any of them had spoken beyond the initial good mornings.

"Yes." Lar'a nodded. "I need to speak with Serihk first, though. Go warm up, and I'll meet you in the gym."

"Okay." Astrid slipped off her seat and left.

Bryant grabbed a piece of toast and stood as well. "I'll leave you to it then."

Once they had gone, Lar'a turned to Serihk.

"I have an idea for what to do with Astrid."

———

SERIHK HAD Lar'a present the idea to Bryant after he spent the day making calls to persuade and negotiate and ensure its viability. He didn't want Bryant to reject it out of hand, and he didn't relish the thought of having his feelings twisted up into something pathetic and grotesque and then thrown in his face again.

He watched, though, and Bryant must have guessed because he sent suspicious glances up at the ceiling as Lar'a began her explanation. He had crossed his arms and stood with his feet planted as though he might have to fight off an assault.

As he listened, his face transformed into something soft with shock. "You can really do that?" Bryant asked when Lar'a finished.

"Serihk has spent the day arranging it," Lar'a said. "But nothing will move forward without your permission. And Astrid's, of course."

Bryant shook his head as a disbelieving smile slowly spread across his lips. "She's going to love it."

"And you?" Lar'a asked.

"Yeah. Yeah, I love it, too. You have my permission."

"Good. I was going to threaten you otherwise." Lar'a grinned, but Serihk knew she wasn't joking, and Bryant's unamused look indicated he knew as well. He didn't comment, though.

"It's about dinner time," he said instead. "Are we telling her now?"

"That's the idea," she replied.

Once they left, Serihk stood from his desk and joined them in the dining room. Bryant glanced at him as he walked in but didn't say anything. He pressed his lips together and looked away. Serihk tried not to feel the disappointment of that. It was petty and selfish and gave credence to Bryant's accusation that he wanted to be a hero.

Astrid came in soon after and hesitated in the doorway when she saw them all standing there. "What's going on?"

Bryant took a seat and nodded for Astrid to do the same. "Sit down. Eat. It's not bad."

"But what is it?" she asked, sitting and putting food on her plate. Lar'a and Serihk sat as well, and Serihk started eating. He was just here to answer questions.

"Lar'a and Serihk have something to tell you," Bryant said. Serihk nodded to Lar'a, and Lar's smiled as she leaned forward.

"Do you remember me talking about the Gat'Raph?"

"Yeah," Astrid said. "You were one."

"That's right. They're the best," Lar'a said, and she

wasn't being arrogant, she was stating a fact. The Gat'Raph was the most effective and highly sought-after warrior order of the Klah'Eel, an empire whose main export was warriors. "They're culturally significant, and they've only ever accepted klah'eel."

Astrid frowned and didn't interrupt.

"The Klah'Eel government wants to improve the integration of non-klah'eel citizens with the majority culture," Lar'a continued. "So, the Gat'Raph are going to start training human children."

Astrid's eyes went wide. "Since when?"

"Since a little after lunch today," Serihk answered, dabbing his lips with his napkin. The major general of the Gat'Raph had been baffled at first, but he'd seen the tactical advantage of diversifying the species of his soldiers and the political advantage of being seen to support one of the government's pet causes. And accepting a handful of experimental recruits wasn't such a huge undertaking for an organization regularly contracted to start and end wars.

Astrid bit her lip. Serihk could see her putting things together, but she looked at them with a wariness that made Serihk think of Bryant. "Human children like me?"

Lar'a grinned. "Human children like you."

"Really?" Astrid leaped from her seat and squealed.

"It's not going to be easy, Astrid," Bryant said quickly. "The Gat'Raph are tough, and most of the other humans will come from powerful political families and elite Human schools."

"Yeah, so they'll be pampered and soft, and I'll kick their asses," Astrid scowled.

Bryant barked out a laugh and shook his head. "That's my girl."

Astrid sat back down and shoved a piece of meat in her

mouth. She looked up at Lar'a with wide and expectant eyes. "Tell me everything I need to know."

Serihk smiled as he finished his dinner and listened to Lar'a hold forth on the first apprentice year of the Gat'Raph, Astrid already chiming in with questions and clarifications. Bryant watched his daughter with a soft smile of his own, and when he caught Serihk's eye, it grew larger. Serihk's heart skipped a beat. It must have shown on his face because Bryant's expression turned a little sly before he looked away and put his glass to his lips.

Serihk guessed how long this conversation could go on, so when he finished his dinner, he nodded to them all and left the room. He was pleased with the solution they'd found. After spending a couple of weeks in Qesha for the Senate meeting, Lar'a and Serihk would take Astrid to Tava with them and hand her off to the Gat'Raph. Serihk was certain she would do well with them, and even if he weren't certain, Lar'a was, and her opinion meant more.

He tried not to think about Bryant disappearing back out into the galaxy tomorrow, away from him and out of his life. Of course, Serihk would keep tabs on Astrid, so it was possible he'd get news of Bryant every once in a while. He might hear if Bryant perhaps settled down, if he found good work. But would Serihk know if he ever found happiness? Would he know if Bryant ever managed to put down whatever crushing burden he carried on his broad shoulders, or if he ever stopped dragging himself through life with one eye looking over his shoulder?

Serihk's life would be easy enough to follow, and he selfishly wondered if Bryant would bother. If he'd see some headline about some counsel meeting and skim the article to see if Serihk's name came up. Serihk grimaced as he forced himself to admit that Bryant had no reason to care. These few days hadn't been for Bryant what they had been for Serihk. Since the moment they met, Serihk had imposed his will and his alone. Serihk had grabbed him that morning, had transferred him to his ship from jail, had made him work with him during the day. No wonder Serihk thought the current situation was perfect; all he ever did was what he wanted, and he expected Bryant to like it and say thank you.

He was halfway down the hallway to his bedroom when he heard heavy footsteps behind him. He turned to see Bryant striding toward him. A flicker of a frown passed over his rugged features, but then it resolved into a look of determination.

"Bryant, what—"

Bryant grabbed his upper arm and the back of his neck and pulled him down into a rough kiss.

Serihk's muscles tensed. His brain stuttered to a stop.

Then Bryant pushed his back against the wall and pressed his body to his, and all the sensations suddenly slammed back into him. The heat of Bryant's skin and the hardness of his muscles. The scratch of his beard. The warm wet of his tongue, dragging along the seam of Serihk's lips. Serihk slid his fingers into Bryant's hair to pull him closer as he opened his mouth under Bryant's insistence.

Goddess, he had wanted this. He moaned. Bryant smiled against his mouth and slipped a muscled thigh between Serihk's legs. Serihk bucked his hips against it with a whine that would have been embarrassing if he'd had the higher brain functioning to care. Bryant's fingers clenched around the muscles in Serihk's arm and the back of his head.

Bryant broke the kiss but kept his body pressing Serihk against the wall. When Serihk tried to chase his lips, Bryant put their foreheads together so that he couldn't reach, but their noses brushed and nudged each other.

"What does the gray mean?" Bryant asked.

"What?" Serihk's heart hammered, and his cock throbbed against the muscle of Bryant's thigh. He didn't have enough blood in his brain to process strange questions.

Bryant let go of his arm and trailed his fingers up Serihk's neck, caressing his throat.

"You had gray stripes all along here a second ago," Bryant said. He dropped his head to kiss Serihk's pulse point and chuckled. "It's all purple now, though, 'cause you want it so bad."

Serihk's breath hitched. Bryant had noticed that? His skin tingled, and he knew the purple had extended up to his temples and into his hairline. He never had been able to control his colors no matter how much training he received. The most he could do was force it down.

Bryant moved to kiss the other side of his throat, fingers still soothing along his skin.

"So what does the gray mean?" he asked again.

Serihk swallowed and bit his lip. "Sadness," he admitted.

Bryant pulled back to press their foreheads together again. He frowned at Serihk, and Serihk tried to look away, but Bryant caught his chin and kept him looking into his eyes. He searched Serihk's face, and Serihk knew his purple was getting tinged with the orange of embarrassment.

"Is that about me too?" Bryant asked.

Serihk twisted a bit, but Bryant was firm, and Serihk didn't really want to get away. He just wanted to stop feeling so exposed.

"Yes," he said quietly. Bryant nodded slowly and then kissed him again, gently and sweetly.

Serihk sank into the kiss. It was so much easier than talking.

The hand Bryant had had on his chin slowly trailed down his chest, parting his robe and then tracing over his belly toward his hips. Serihk inhaled sharply, and Bryant nipped his lower lip before he dropped his hand down to palm Serihk's cock.

"Bryant——" Serihk gasped, but Bryant covered his mouth again with a kiss and started rubbing him through his pants. Serihk couldn't stop the little gasps and grunts as Bryant rubbed him, his mind spiraling and swirling. His legs quivered, and he grabbed Bryant's shoulders to keep himself upright. He tried to twitch his hips into the pressure, but Bryant eased off when he did, and he whined. "Bryant."

"I wonder if I could make your whole body purple," Bryant said with a chuckle, and he nosed up Serihk's neck and nipped at his throat. Serihk shuddered. "We got one more night to try." He dropped his hands to Serihk's hips and pulled them against his own, and Serihk felt the rock-hard ridge of his cock. "Come to my bed."

Serihk shook his head. "No," he said, and Bryant immediately let go, eyes widening horribly, but Serihk grabbed his sides and stopped him from stepping back. "I want you in mine. I want to finally see what you look like there."

Even if it was just once. Even if he was signing himself up for emotional torture every time he went to bed until he was eventually, miraculously over this infatuation, if that ever happened.

Bryant's face cleared, and the side of his mouth lifted

in a smile. "You been thinking about that a lot? About what I'd look like in your bed?"

Serihk flicked some flex metal out of the molding beside their feet and started wrapping it loosely up Bryant's ankle and calf, more a suggestion than anything else. Bryant's eyes widened when the metal touched his skin, and Serihk had a perfect view of his pupils dilating.

"What do you think?"

Bryant swallowed and licked his lips. He stepped back. "I think lead the way."

Serihk smirked and grabbed Bryant's wrist. He pulled him the rest of the way down the hallway, his arousal settling to a low hum in his belly but his heart pounding with anticipation. Bryant was easily strong enough to break Serihk's grip, but he let himself be pulled along and yanked into the room when Serihk got the door open.

As the door closed, Serihk spun Bryant around and stepped in close to get chest to chest and make the most of his height advantage. He slid a hand up Bryant's neck, to the back of his head, and tilted his face to look up at him. Bryant's lips parted, his pupil's still blown wide.

"I want to take care of you tonight," Serihk murmured. He tugged Bryant's hair lightly between his fingers and smoothed a thumb along his bearded jaw. "I want to make you feel so good you can't think anymore."

"Yeah?" Bryant asked breathlessly.

"Yeah," Serihk whispered in his ear and then kissed the hollow behind it. He felt Bryant shiver. "Will you let me do that?"

Bryant let out a shuddery breath. "Fuck yes. Anything you want."

Serihk smiled against his ear and dropped his hand to the front of Bryant's pants. He crawled flex metal along the floor and felt the way Bryant's cock twitched when it reached his ankles and started winding up his legs, firm and tight this time, much more than a mere suggestion. "Good."

Serihk stepped to the side and circled the big man slowly. He ran one hand up his strong core and his broad chest, up to his throat, and dropped the other to cup his balls through the fabric. Bryant leaned back into him, and when Serihk pulled Bryant's lower lip down with two of his fingers, Bryant let his mouth drop open. Serihk thrust them into his mouth, and Bryant let out a moan and started sucking them.

"That's right," Serihk murmured, giving his balls a squeeze. "Don't stop."

Serihk nuzzled into Bryant's neck and inhaled deeply as his tentacles crawled up Bryant's body. Serihk had *wanted* this. The smell of Bryant, his warm, solid body against his. To hear him sigh, to feel him give in. Serihk thrusted his fingers slowly as he kissed Bryant's neck and set his tentacles to peeling off their clothes.

Bryant moaned around Serihk's fingers when the flex metal finally tightened around his wrists, and Serihk nipped his ear.

"I've got you. I've got all of you," Serihk whispered. Once their clothes had fallen to the floor, Serihk pulled Bryant back into his chest so they were skin to skin. Humans ran so hot, the feel of Bryant burned into Serihk, and Serihk tightened his grip to get more of that overwhelming feeling and pressed his length into the cleft of Bryant's ass. Bryant shuddered and canted his hips back against him, making Serihk hiss and bite the muscle of his shoulder.

Serihk laved his tongue over his bite and looked down Bryant's muscular chest to his hard cock and the precum beading on the head. Hard and near dripping just from being tied up and stripped and having Serihk fondle his balls and finger fuck his mouth. How much harder could he get without a touch on his cock, Serihk wondered.

"You should see yourself," Serihk breathed in his ear and watched the flush bloom over Bryant's chest. He nibbled along the shell of his ear. "Get over here."

Serihk pulled Bryant around but let his flex metal tentacles do most of the work of pushing Bryant, stumbling, to the bed. Serihk stopped him at the foot of it and stepped behind him again. He kissed the nape of Bryant's neck as the flex metal around Bryant's wrists pulled his arms behind his back, and then Serihk knocked his feet wider apart.

Serihk grabbed Bryant's hips, so warm in his hands, and then growled in Bryant's ear, "Bend over. I've wanted to do this for a long time."

Serihk pushed between Bryant's shoulder blades and on the nape of his neck, and Bryant went easily, pressing his chest down on the bed, his ass raised in the air. He was breathing hard, his muscular back expanding on each inhale, his thighs quivering.

Serihk smoothed a hand down his spine. "I've got you."

Bryant let out a shaky sigh. "I know."

A dangerous coil of overwhelming affection threatened to choke Serihk, and he dropped to his knees before he could analyze it. He had his fantasy spread out before him. He should focus on that.

He grabbed the back of Bryant's thighs and laved a tongue over his balls. Bryant's entire body jerked, and he let out a yelp. Serihk smirked and teased the tip of his tongue against Bryant's taint. He enjoyed the feel of Bryant squirming as the full-bodied taste of his musk flooded his mouth.

"Oh fuck, Serihk," Bryant groaned, and with a moan, Serihk finally let himself have what he'd been wanting.

He dug his fingers into the meat of Bryant's thighs and sucked on his balls. Serihk filled his mouth with them, rolling them on his tongue, licking at their seam. He wrapped some of his tentacles around Bryant's ankles and pulled them farther apart to expose him more and give Serihk better access.

Bryant writhed and whimpered, and a drop of precum dripped off his cock, which hung heavy between his thighs. But Serihk ignored it. Instead, he licked broad strokes backward, away from Bryant's balls.

Bryant gasped. "Oh god. Serihk, you—"

"Shhh." Serihk soothed his thumbs over Bryant's hips and tightened the flex metal around Bryant's wrists to hold him still. Bryant tensed against the metal, testing it, and then dropped back heavily into the bed.

When he was loose and pliant again, Serihk leaned back, took the two globes of Bryant's ass in his hands, and spread them. Bryant whimpered, and Serihk watched that tight pucker twitch. There were so many things he wanted to see disappear into that tight hole. Flex metal, his fingers, his cock. Serihk had to close his eyes as a hard pulse of pleasure went through him at the thought. He would fuck Bryant's hole soon, but first, he leaned forward and tongued it.

Bryant cried out, and his hips twisted, and Serihk wondered if anyone had ever eaten him out in the way he so clearly deserved, but he wasn't going to stop and ask. Serihk teased Bryant's hole with the tip of his tongue, fluttering it back and forth, dipping inside and catching on the rim. When Bryant's hips twitched toward him and his panting breaths sounded more like whines, Serihk stopped his teasing. He buried his face in Bryant's ass and ate him out with open-mouthed enthusiasm. Serihk groaned against Bryant's hole at the feel of Bryant's whole body shaking. He could practically taste Bryant's war between his shame and his desperation in the way he alternated trying to chase Serihk's tongue with his ass and trying to twist his hips away. Serihk's cock throbbed, knowing that Bryant was letting him do this to him.

Serihk dropped his hand to his length and gave himself a few pulls as he licked and sucked on Bryant's pucker. He moaned as Bryant shifted and changed position slightly. Serihk replaced his mouth with the pad of his finger, rubbing little circles against Bryant's rim as he ducked his head and looked up through Bryant's spread legs. Bryant had managed to lift himself up enough to brace his shoulder against the bed to look down at Serihk behind him.

His eyes were wide and his mouth open and panting as he took in Serihk on his knees with one finger against Bryant's hole and his hand on his own cock. Serihk smirked and kept their eyes locked as he licked from Bryant's taint to his balls.

"Oh god, Serihk."

"I could come just from the taste of you." Serihk gave himself a few more strokes and spoke with his lips against the skin of Bryant's sack. He let his eyes roll back with the pleasure. "I think I might. Just get myself off and leave you here for when I'm ready again."

Bryant closed his eyes, and his hole twitched against Serihk's finger. "Oh fuck, Serihk."

Serihk gave Bryant's balls one more kiss and stood back up. "But I promised I'd take care of you."

His flex metal pulled open his bedside drawer and pulled out a jar of lube. He scooped a generous amount onto one of his fingers and abruptly slid it into Bryant's hole up to the knuckle.

Bryant let out a choked sound that quickly morphed into a low moan as Serihk fingered him. Serihk watched his digit disappear inside Bryant's body for a few thrusts, eyes glued to the way his entrance stretched and contracted around Serihk's invading finger.

Then Serihk pulled it out and called a few particularly strong tentacles to pull Bryant up onto the bed proper and flip him onto his back.

Bryant's eyes lit at the manhandling.

Serihk smiled and made sure the remaining tentacles around Bryant's wrists and ankles remained tight and stretched him long. They pulled Bryant's arms over his head so that the muscles of his shoulders bunched and pulled his ankles to either corner of the bed to keep him exposed.

Serihk paused before climbing onto the bed after him, caught by the look in Bryant's eyes. They were hazy with pleasure, eager, desperate, and shameless. And they watched Serihk with anticipation and trust. So much trust, Serihk felt the now familiar need to protect surging through his arousal. He climbed onto the bed, leaned over Bryant, and put his hand on his cheek. He stroked his thumb over Bryant's cheekbones, and Bryant smiled slow and easy in a way Serihk had never seen.

Serihk's heart clenched painfully. Bryant was only offering him this one night. He'd made it very clear. And now that he was living it, Serihk knew with absolute and utter certainty that this wouldn't be enough. Having this one night and no others would wreck him and haunt him for years.

Bryant frowned. "Serihk, you're turning gray."

Serihk shook his head hard, furious with himself for letting that feeling creep out.

"No, no, I'm fine."

Before Bryant could call it out again, Serihk dragged his fingers up Bryant's inner thighs to his still-slick opening and pumped two fingers into him.

Bryant arched and cried out, his eyes closing. "Oh fuck, Serihk."

Serihk found the soft, spongy spot he was looking for and stroked it firmly, and Bryant keened and arched again. Serihk slid a strong tentacle around Bryant's middle and held him back down.

"That's it." Serihk stroked that spot and tangled his hands in Bryant's hair. "That's it."

Bryant opened his eyes and met Serihk's gaze. He kept his eyes locked to Serihk's as Serihk stroked faster and pressed harder, even as he panted and twisted and whimpered. Serihk steeled himself against that look but felt himself slipping. He wanted to kiss him. He wanted to hold him. The man had lain himself out like a feast and, greedy bastard that Serihk was, he wanted *more*.

Serihk thrust in a third finger without warning, and Bryant shouted.

"Oh god, Serihk. I want—" He whined when Serihk ground down on that spot, just to see him dissolve into anguished pleasure.

"What do you want?"

"I want you to fuck me," Bryant managed. He gritted his teeth and stared down Serihk with a determination that would have looked more at home on a battlefield than in a bedroom, but that made Serihk's balls draw up tight. "*You*. I want *you* inside me."

Serihk dropped his forehead to Bryant's shoulder with

a groan. His heart was going to be shattered by the morning.

Three fingers still buried inside Bryant, Serihk caught Bryant's jaw with his free hand and kissed him. He didn't know if the low, reverberating moan came from him or Bryant, but he didn't care as Bryant yielded for him, melting up into him, his lips soft, pliant, and eager. They parted at the barest brush of his tongue, and Serihk slipped his tongue into Bryant's mouth to mirror the thrusting of his fingers.

He kept his mouth on Bryant's as he reluctantly pulled his fingers free. Bryant whined and canted his hips, but his breath hitched when Serihk settled himself between his thick thighs. Serihk sat up and lubed himself generously, head falling back at the feel of his hand on his hypersensitive cock. Then he put a hand on either of Bryant's thighs and spread them wider. He dragged the head of his cock over Bryant's twitching opening, savoring the look of desperation on Bryant's face. Then he slowly pushed inside. He heard Bryant's low groan, but Serihk had to squeeze his eyes shut against the searing, overwhelming pleasure before he came too early.

*Oh goddess.*

Oh fuck.

The man was tight. Hot, tight, silky smooth, and still whimpering and shaking.

"Oh Bryant," Serihk murmured, opening his eyes and leaning forward to cover him with his body. He wound flex metal around Bryant's thighs to hold him open for him and braced himself on one elbow next to Bryant's head to give himself a good view and better leverage. Bryant looked down at their joined bodies, and Serihk followed his gaze to watch himself sinking into him. Serihk thrust, dragging out and feeling the tight grip of Bryant's rim on his cock, and then pushing back in and feeling Bryant yield and give.

"Yes," Bryant hissed. "Fuck, yes."

Serihk sped up, invading and stretching Bryant with long, deep strokes. He lightly scratched the nails of his free hand down Bryant's chest and watched Bryant track its progress down to his own cock. Bryant's lips parted, and when Serihk finally took hold of Bryant's weeping length, Bryant dropped his head back against the pillow with a growl.

Serihk changed his angle to brush that spot inside Bryant on each stroke and make Bryant's hips jerk and push his cock into Serihk's fist. Soon Bryant's hips were rocking with his, ass slapping against Serihk's hip bones, and his cock thrusting up into the circle of Serihk's fingers.

But Serihk's own edge marched closer and closer. He couldn't hold out much longer. He tightened his grip on Bryant's cock and started stroking along with his thrusts. He needed to see Bryant come undone, to feel him spasming around his cock. He needed to *feel* what the man let Serihk do to him.

"Oh god, oh god," Bryant gasped. He stared up into Serihk's face, brows pinched, lips parted, and arms straining against his bonds.

Serihk pressed his forehead against his. "Come for me, Bryant," he huskily demanded, and Bryant's hips stuttered.

"I—fuck. I—"

Serihk rubbed his thumb over Bryant's slick cockhead and dropped his lips to his ear. "Come for me."

Bryant threw his head back with a cry, and his cock pulsed against Serihk's palm.

Serihk pulled on him mercilessly and watched the cum shoot up Bryant's chest. His muscles clenched down around Serihk.

Serihk groaned and pounded into him, trying to reach that peak that was getting closer and closer.

"Bryant!" He hit it and crashed over it, pleasure and warmth spilling down his thighs as he shot his spend deep into Bryant's hole. He pumped a few more times and then collapsed on top of him and buried his face in Bryant's neck.

Serihk lay there, panting and shuddering as the last waves of pleasure receded, feeling the bulk of the human pinned beneath him. He tried to capture the feeling, define it, articulate it, file it away so he could revisit it in the future. He tried to hold on to this even though he knew it would all slip through his memory like water through his fingers until he was left with only the shallowest of recollections.

Finally, he sighed and rolled off Bryant's body to lay next to him. He slowly unwound the tentacles around Bryant's wrists and ankles and pulled them back into the wall. After a moment to gather the energy, he sat up and turned to Bryant, who still lay there in a daze. He massaged the red marks around his wrists, working the blood back into them.

Bryant winced as he stretched his arms up. "Shoulders are sore."

"I'm sure." Serihk dug his thumbs into the bunched muscles and then gently helped Bryant lower his arms down. "Take it easy. Just lie here."

He pressed a hand into the center of Bryant's chest to emphasize his instruction and then dragged himself off the bed and into the en suite. He wet a towel with warm water.

"You're gonna clean me off and everything?" Bryant asked with a crooked smile, still rubbing his wrists, as Serihk returned.

"Well, you're a mess," Serihk replied with a chuckle,

even though he wasn't joking. Cum was splattered up Bryant's belly and chest and leaked out his hole. His cock still glistened with the lube from Serihk's palm. "Let me."

Bryant moved his arms out of the way and lay still as Serihk leaned over him and wiped him clean. He blinked when the towel first touched his skin.

"It's warm."

"Of course it is."

Serihk finished the cleanup, gave Bryant's balls a last affectionate squeeze that made him inhale sharply, and then tossed the towel away. He glanced back down and found Bryant looking up at him, eyes soft and sleepy. Serihk licked his lips. He was already going to be heart-broken in the morning, what was a little more?

He cupped Bryant's jaw and kissed him again, sweet and gentle. He half-expected Bryant to turn away or push him off now that the main event was over, but he didn't.

Bryant grabbed the back of Serihk's neck with one hand and his hip with the other and pulled him down against his body. He tangled his fingers in Serihk's hair, and they kissed languidly, skin sliding together, limbs tangling. Neither was young enough to get hard again so soon, but that made the warm pleasure of their bodies sliding together all the more indulgent.

"Stay here tonight?" Serihk whispered against Bryant's lips when they parted. He tried not to let his eyes give away how desperately he wanted the answer to be yes, and he hoped the swirls on his skin were still purple and hadn't gone gray.

Bryant bumped his nose against Serihk's and kissed him again. "Okay."

So Serihk pulled the blankets over them, wrapped the human up in his arms, and tried to enjoy the feel of him instead of dreading the morning.

## Chapter Five

BRYANT WOKE LAZILY, comfortably. Warm and wrapped in soft blankets that weren't his—

His heart lurched, and he sat up with a gasp. It took him a moment to remember where he was, eyes darting wildly around unfamiliar surroundings, his heart beating too fast to think.

Serihk's room.

Serihk's bed.

Bryant dropped back onto the pillows with a groan. He dragged the heels of his palms down his face. To wake so slowly and sleep so deeply in such an unfamiliar place was liable to get him killed. This was why he had to leave and why he had to leave today. This place was making him soft. *Serihk* was making him soft.

He rolled onto his stomach to reach the edge of the huge bed and drag himself out of it but stopped with his cheek pressed against the soft sheets. It was *nice*, and he wasn't going to get anything nice out there, not for a long time. He nosed into the nearest pillow and inhaled deeply, filling his nose with Serihk's scent. Clean, expensive, arousing. He should forget that smell. It made him too relaxed and he couldn't afford that. His edge was all he had. It was all Astrid had.

Except, it wasn't anymore.

Bryant pulled the covers up over his head and cocooned himself in the smell of Serihk and sex to hold off the day for just a little longer.

Astrid was going to be taken care of. She was going somewhere safe and secure that would give her a future. Astrid had more now. She didn't need his edge. She didn't need him watching every corner, playing every angle, staying as sharp as a razor blade.

Bryant jumped at the sound of the door opening but then heard Serihk's tread and relaxed again. He suddenly felt ridiculous curled up in bed like a child. Serihk would have seen that he was awake too, seen him pull the covers over his head. He was always watching.

If he stayed where he was, would Serihk come to wake him anyway? Would he kiss him again, or was that just for fucking and foreplay? Lots of men liked to kiss while they fucked, and even after, while they were still feeling giddy from it, but then didn't want to kiss during the day. Bryant didn't usually want to kiss during the day, but he didn't usually feel this way about his partners either. He'd never felt this way about anyone.

It was probably just that he hadn't had sex in so long and that he'd never had sex that good. Being a single father and a criminal to boot didn't give him many opportunities for intimate encounters, even hurried ones in back alleys. Of course he'd feel things for the first man to take him to bed in years.

But it wasn't just that, and he knew it. And he already felt bad for reducing proud, vulnerable, clever Serihk—

who fixed the galaxy's problems and then Bryant's as well —to just a man who took him to bed.

When Serihk set something on the table, Bryant sat up and pushed the covers off. He didn't want to wait to see if Serihk would come to him; there was too much risk of disappointment. Serihk was already dressed, which meant he'd woken, gotten ready, and left the room while Bryant slumbered on, and that reminder of how vulnerable he'd made himself made Bryant's stomach clench coldly. Too soft.

But then he saw the contents of the tray Serihk had set down and forgot his self-loathing for a moment.

"Is that a cinnamon roll?" He swung his legs out of bed and padded over. He remembered his nakedness when Serihk's eyes widened and swept over him appreciatively, purple curling up the sides of his neck. Bryant would miss the way Serihk looked at him. He smiled crookedly back at Serihk and openly admired his elegant, tall form. Bryant had never seen a man look so beautiful and so powerful at the same time.

"Indeed it is." Serihk recovered quickly and passed him the small plate. "I love a little symmetry. And you and Astrid seemed to like them."

"You wanna try a bite this time?" Bryant peeled off a piece that had just the right amount of frosting.

Serihk hesitated and then reached for the piece Bryant held. "Alright."

Bryant bypassed his hand and stepped in close to bring it to his lips instead. Serihk's eyes widened, but he opened his mouth and let Bryant feed it to him. Bryant smirked and smoothed his thumb along Serihk's lips. Serihk flicked his tongue out to lick a dollop of frosting off the pad of his thumb, and Bryant inhaled sharply.

The man wasn't nearly as guarded as he seemed. He

was so open with Bryant, and Bryant could see every want and desire written on his face and in his eyes. This brilliant man influenced empires and ended wars, and he shuddered when Bryant touched his lips. When he saw a starburst of gray at Serihk's temple, he had to look away.

He stepped back and picked up the coffee cup. "Is Astrid up?"

Serihk let out a deep breath, and the color receded back down his neck, leaving him smooth and pale. He took a sip of his vile Qeshian concoction and leaned his hip against the table.

"Already demanding Lar'a give her some more lessons so that she won't be behind her cohort."

"That sounds right." Bryant nodded and shoved a piece of fluffy bread and icing in his mouth. He closed his eyes to savor as he chewed and imagined Serihk watching him as he did. The thought sent a thrill down to his cock, and despite his misgivings, he wondered if they could fuck one more time before they got to port. "Thank you, by the way."

"For?"

"Everything. But especially for taking care of Astrid." The tight knot of fear and anxiety that had lived in Bryant's chest from the moment a screaming baby girl was dropped into his filthy arms wasn't going to loosen so easily or so quickly, but Bryant picked at it enough to get the next words out. "She's everything to me. What you've done for her, the chance you've given her…it's more than I could ever do, and I can't thank you enough."

Serihk cupped Bryant's jaw, and Bryant closed his mouth. Serihk looked at him seriously.

"You don't give yourself enough credit," he said. "You raised a strong and resilient young woman, and she's earned this opportunity. What I did was trivial."

Serihk waited until Bryant nodded slowly, and then he ran his thumb along his cheekbone and dropped his hands.

They went back to their breakfasts in silence while Bryant let the minor emotional wound he'd just opened up scab over. He tried to enjoy the quiet, the food, the easy presence of Serihk by his side, and the growing arousal of being naked just an arm's length away from him. He was halfway through the roll when Serihk spoke again.

"Have you given any more thought to staying on as my consultant?"

The warm feelings fled.

Bryant sighed and let himself finish his roll. Then he licked his fingers and nodded. "I have."

"And?" Serihk's expression was dignified and regal, and Bryant could tell from the complete lack of color in his face that it was entirely constructed.

"And I don't think it's right for me." Bryant turned away to start hunting down his clothes, so he didn't have to see whatever Serihk's face did next. He found them folded neatly on an armchair in the corner, and his throat ached. Of course the man would fold his damn clothes.

"Why not?" Serihk's cup clinked as he set it down. Bryant scowled to himself as he started pulling on his clothes. The only thing that would make this conversation worse would be to do it naked.

"It's cushy," he replied.

"What's wrong with cushy?"

"It'll make me soft."

"What's wrong with being soft?"

Bryant exhaled hard through his nose and turned around fully dressed, frustration and pain making him snap. "What's wrong with being soft is that when you get tired of me and you kick me back out onto the streets, it'll kill me."

Serihk's mouth dropped open, and Bryant didn't give him a chance to collect himself.

"Do you get that? *This* is dangerous for me." Bryant stomped toward him and gestured between them. "Because *this* makes me feel safe, and I'm fucking not. It'll make me lazy, and I'll get complacent, and then when I go back out there, I'll end up dead. So I need to leave."

He spun around to make for the door, but flex metal wrapped around his upper arm and yanked him back.

"That's what this is about?" Serihk demanded, standing rigid with his tentacle wrapped around Bryant's bicep. Red flooded up his throat. "You're afraid of not being afraid anymore?"

"Don't make me sound absurd," Bryant growled.

"It *is* absurd," Serihk cried and clenched his fists. "You're finally safe, so you'll throw yourself back out into danger because you think you'll end up there anyway?"

"I *know* I will."

"You don't *know* anything. Just—"

"Fuck you," Bryant yelled, something exploding in his chest. "Let me go. Just because you get to manhandle me in bed doesn't mean you get to do it out here."

Serihk flinched back, and the flex metal slithered off.

"*I* will decide what I do, not you," Bryant snapped. This time, he did make it to the door, then out into the hall. He fumed back to his room, and when his own door finally slid shut behind him, he let out the frustrated snarl that had been building behind his teeth. He sat heavily down on the bed and put his head in his hands.

He was going to be seeing Serihk's stricken look whenever he closed his eyes for a long time. He lifted his head and looked around at the comfortable furniture, the soft furnishings, the dark wood. It had been a lovely vacation, and the thing he was going to remember the most was the

hurt and confusion on Serihk's face as Bryant yelled
at him.

But he couldn't pin his life on Serihk's goodwill. Serihk
might like him now, might want him in his bed and even—
confusingly—in his study working with him. But it was all
ludicrous. A man like Serihk didn't need a man like Bryant
—it was odd enough that he wanted him—and Bryant
couldn't put himself in a situation where he needed Serihk.
That sort of one-way dependency would leave Bryant
ruined and worse off than he was before.

He pulled at his hair. He was already worse off than he
was before, though, because now when he was miserable,
he would know what it felt like to be comforted.

He glanced at the baseboards, thinking about what was
hidden inside. Serihk was everywhere here. He was the
whole ship, really. Bryant stood and put his hand against
the wall. That was probably why it felt so safe. He hadn't
been so watched over since they had first settled in Carta
and his mother had slept between him and the door.

Bryant made a fist and banged it gently against the
wall. And in two years, she was dead. Because good things
always ended, and the best-intentioned people let you
down. He started grabbing the things he had managed to
scatter throughout the room in just a few days. Clothes,
some spare parts for his tablet, his coat.

He looked at the candelabra sitting on his bedside
table. He looked at it sometimes before bed, ruminating on
the odd feeling of being gifted something so extraordinary.
Which always then made him ruminate on the
extraordinary man that had given it to him. He shook his
head. He would not be taking that with him.

He turned to the playing cards still strewn about on the
table from a game with Astrid. He started to gather them
into a deck and then paused. When would he ever get to

play cards with Astrid again? When would he even see her again? He covered his mouth with his hand. Never again, if she were lucky. If everything went according to plan, she wouldn't have any reason to associate with a poor refugee probably back on the wrong side of the law, probably with enemies. Hell, he had enemies right now.

If he worked with the Qeshian emissary, though...

God, what was he doing? What the hell was he doing? What was the point of it all? For the longest time, the point had been Astrid: to keep her alive, to keep her safe, to give her a *chance*. And before that, the point had been to keep himself alive.

Well, Astrid was fine, and Bryant was still alive, so now what? What was the point if he still couldn't sleep a full night, couldn't enjoy warm beds, or cinnamon rolls in the morning, or drinks in the evening with someone that made him giddy and excited in a way he'd never felt before?

He'd rather have alone forever than even just months with a man like Serihk?

If his options were miserable now or miserable later, why was he choosing miserable now?

Bryant started storming to the door and came up short when Serihk opened it.

He looked momentarily surprised to see Bryant face-to-face with him, but he recovered quickly. He held out a tablet.

"I've drafted a contract." He stepped forward and pushed the tablet into Bryant's hands. "It's a two-year position. Your salary would be paid by the empire, not me. They'd also cover protection, benefits, and housing in case you decide to work on-planet. You would be free to terminate the contract for any reason, but we could not terminate it except in some extreme circumstances. It favors you heavily."

Bryant frowned and looked down at the screen in his hands. It was filled with tight, tiny script in Universal, all Qeshian legalese, but Bryant didn't doubt Serihk's honesty. He looked back up at Serihk's pale face. Bryant wished he wouldn't do that. He wanted to see Serihk's feelings, because his own were getting complicated and confusing.

"I don't understand."

"It wasn't fair of me to expect you to risk so much on my word or my whim," Serihk said. He stood tense. His hands were unclenched, but they twitched. "You deserve more security and more certainty. This gives you that."

He gestured to the tablet, then clasped his hands behind his back and straightened, but he worried his lower lip with his teeth.

"If I—" Serihk started, then licked his lips. "If we—you don't need me with that, is the point. So if there is a we—if you want there to be a we—it's not connected to your personal and financial security. They're separate."

Bryant looked back down at the contract and nodded slowly. He stared at it a moment, but his head was too full to read it. Serihk had understood. Of course he had understood. And of course he had bent over backward for Bryant.

"You did this because you want me to take the consulting job?"

"Yes." Serihk nodded. "I think you'd be an asset, and I don't want you to deny yourself safety and security because you don't have any control and you don't trust me. Which I don't blame you for at all because it is entirely reasonable given our very brief acquaintance."

Bryant nodded and tapped his finger on the edge of the tablet. He could feel his body vibrating as he slowly, slowly started to acknowledge the possibility of an entirely new life. "And if I did take this, you'd still be interested in whatever it is we're doing?"

Serihk stepped forward and took Bryant's jaw in his hands. The touch startled him, but the cool pads of Serihk's fingers sent soft little tingles across his skin. "Yes. By the Goddess, yes."

Bryant could have this. He could have this and so much more. Astrid was safe. He could be safe. He could be warm and happy and have companionship. And he could help people. He could think outside of himself for once. He'd never even thought of doing that before. Helping himself had seemed impossible enough.

Bryant grabbed Serihk's wrists. "I want all of it. If I'm doing this, I want all of it. I want to help fix Tava and the fucked-up situation my people are in. I want to make a difference." He swallowed. "And I want to stay with you. I want you to hold me. I want you to kiss me—"

Serihk pulled his face up and slotted their mouths together. Bryant groaned and leaned into him without hesitation.

"Anything. I'll give you anything," Serihk murmured against his lips and then captured them again.

And this time, the feel of Serihk surrounding him, his attention and the pleasure, didn't feel like a treat, or a reprieve, or a distraction. It felt like a beginning.

# Chapter Six

FROM THE MOMENT Bryant pressed his thumb to the tablet and sealed the contract with his print, the day blurred before his eyes.

Serihk had swept him up into another hungry kiss, his face swirling with purple and pink, but then he'd whirled away, his robes flaring out behind him as he rushed to make arrangements.

Bryant packed the rest of his things in a daze before searching for Astrid. He'd found her panting and bright-eyed in the gym with Lar'a and she'd squealed with joy when he'd told her that he'd be staying with Serihk for the foreseeable future.

A tide of guilt lapped at Bryant's heart at the clear relief just behind her delight. She'd been scared for him. More than scared. She was old enough to worry about others now and he never wanted her to have to worry about him. He'd do better; he swore it to himself.

He'd kissed the top of her head and then accepted a surprising – and very sweaty – hug from Lar'a. He frowned at her as she pulled back and ruffled his hair. "You don't mind?"

"That you're staying?" Lar'a raised her horned eyebrows and then snorted a laugh. "Not at all. I'd have minded if you left and I'd had to deal with Serihk moping about for who knows how long." The guilty tide lapped a little higher up on Bryant's heart as he imagined Serihk sitting in one of the lavish chairs in his library with a crystal glass in his hand and gray snaking up around his throat. Lar'a sighed as she racked a weight. "He's going to be difficult enough on Tava without a broken heart on top of it."

Bryant's curiosity broke through his guilt. "Why is he going to be difficult on Tava?"

But then the port docking announcement echoed through the hallways and Lar'a had left Astrid and Bryant to gather their things. As soon as Bryant had carried Astrid's things to his own room, the ship lurched as they docked and servants appeared in the doorway.

With barely a word, the brisk qeshian servants grabbed their bags and ushered them to the main entrance. Then Bryant got his first ever view of Qesha.

He froze at the top of the gangway and stared.

Skyscrapers burst from the ground everywhere around him, climbing up so high he had to crane his neck to see their tops. They glinted in the sunlight, their metal and glass facades reflecting the blue of the sky and the white of passing clouds. Transports whizzed in thick, orderly lines between the huge buildings, flowing through the metropolis like blood vessels.

Bryant jumped as the servant behind him cleared his throat with obvious impatience. Astrid found his hand and he pulled her down the gangway with him, holding her up as she stumbled over her own feet while staring at the skyline. They loaded into a transport and took off to join the rush of other vehicles in the stratosphere of the city.

Before Bryant could get a handle on where they were, how far up they were flying, and how far away they were leaving the docks behind, they were on the top of one of the tallest buildings around and the servants were unloading their bags and carrying them inside. Without so much as a perfunctory tour around the posh, sprawling apartment, the servants showed both Bryant and Astrid to their rooms, dropped off their bags, and disappeared.

Bryant was left standing in the middle of a bedroom three times as large as the hovel he'd lived in with Astrid on Carta, all alone and afraid his skin would leave a stain on his pristine surroundings.

He worried his lip and crossed his arms.

The room was beautiful – lighter than the dark wood interior of the ship but just as luxurious, with a wall of windows that looked out across the shining rows of buildings – but it was sterile. Empty. Charmless.

It wasn't Serihk's.

Bryant knew he should be thankful for his expensive, beautiful room and his privacy but he hadn't agreed to stay because he cared about any of that. He'd agreed to stay because he cared about Serihk and he cared about the man Serihk made him feel like he could be.

And Serihk wasn't here.

Bryant tightened his arms over his chest and ran the side of his thumbnail over his bicep, feeling a little disappointed, a little confused, and a little embarrassed. He'd thought they'd share a room. He *wanted* to share a room and he thought Serihk did too but maybe that had been foolish. Maybe that was a step too far too soon.

The tide of guilt rose up higher on Bryant's heart.

Bryant didn't know what Serihk wanted because he never asked him.

Bryant dropped his head to his chest. He was going to be a terrible partner to this man. Why had Serihk even chosen him? It was ridiculous. The two of them in a loving, healthy relationship between equals?

Bryant shuffled to a chair in the corner, far from the sterile bed and the window that gave him vertigo, and fell heavily down onto it. He wondered again why a man like Serihk wanted anything to do with a man like him. A man who's entire existence could be summed up in his crooked nose and the contents of the threadbare duffle now sitting in the center of the floor.

Bryant rubbed his temples and clenched his jaw. He was going to do better. For Astrid, for Serihk, for himself, for everyone else he was suddenly – miraculously – more fortunate than, he was going to do better.

But without Serihk, he wasn't quite sure where to begin.

Astrid was happily ensconced in her new room with Serihk's series of old adventure books, so Bryant left her to it and sat alone in his room.

The hours clicked by.

Eventually, Bryant dragged himself from his chair and through a hot shower which he was sure felt amazing but that he couldn't enjoy while his throat was clogged with things to say to a man that wasn't there.

After his shower, he returned to a tablet full of notifications for documents he'd gotten clearance to read now that his contract had gone through. He dressed in clothes that felt out of place in the white room and settled down to reading, intent on at least being useful.

More hours clicked by.

The sun went down but the sky outside the huge window hardly darkened, lit by the city as easily as it had been by daylight.

Bryant had just set his tablet aside, rubbed his bleary eyes, and wondered if Serihk even lived in this apartment when he heard the soft click of a door closing. He frowned. Astrid shouldn't be awake at this time. He padded quietly to his own door and opened it to look out into the hall.

The room at the far end – a room Bryant hadn't dared to look in because he hadn't dared to look in any room that wasn't his or Astrid's – had a soft white light shining through the crack in the bottom. Bryant rolled his shoulders back and approached it, his stomach fluttering with the thought of seeing Serihk again and the disappointment that Serihk hadn't come to see him.

He knocked softly and after a moment he heard the unmistakable rustle of robes and the door opened to reveal Serihk's tall, elegant body.

When Serihk's dark eyes fell on Bryant, a swirl of pink appeared on his sharp cheekbones and the hint of black along his neck receded down below his collar. His lips quirked into a smile even as his brows furrowed. "Bryant. I thought you'd be asleep by now."

"I was waiting for you." Bryant crossed his arms over his chest, a little embarrassed to be admitting it but trying to push the embarrassment away. He raised his own eyebrows. "You couldn't see me through your sensors?"

Serihk shook his head, then stepped aside and gestured for Bryant to enter the room. "No, I'm afraid I don't have the apartment fitted with the same security system I have on the ship. I'm just a normal man here."

Bryant barked a quiet laugh and shot Serihk a fond

smile as he stepped into the room. "You're not a normal man anywhere, Serihk."

Starbursts of pink burst on Serihk's cheeks and Bryant's chest warmed.

As he looked around the room, the warmth twisted into longing. *This* was Serihk's bedroom. It was neat and tidy but it had none of the sterility of the room Bryant had been put in. Bookshelves lined one wall, a huge bed with soft-looking sheets sat in the center, and on the other side was a desk full of data tablets with a big screen mounted above it.

Currently, half that screen was dominated by the professional headshot of a blonde, strikingly pretty young man with an arrogant smile. Bryant cocked his head and walked over to the screen. "Who is that?"

"The enemy," Serihk replied in a low voice as he joined Bryant. "Oliver Turner. Second son of the Turner family, and my main concern on Tava."

Bryant frowned up at the image. The young man dripped money and power but looking closely at his hazel eyes, Bryant thought he could detect familiar hints of hunger and desperation. He wanted something, and Bryant didn't think it was just the factory contracts the Turner Corporation was officially in negotiation for.

He opened his mouth to ask Serihk if he was missing something when his eyes fell on a cloth parcel taking up the seat of the desk chair. He'd have thought nothing of the sumptuously wrapped package except that from his angle he could just barely make out the crisp white tag attached to it with the name 'Harrison' written in neat universal. He stepped around the high-backed chair to take a closer look. "What's that?"

When Serihk didn't answer right away, Bryant glanced

up to see that he had completely cleared his skin and clasped his hands behind his back. Bryant's stomach plummeted and the guilty tide that had been rising and rising finally closed over his heart.

Serihk was nervous. He was nervous about how Bryant would react and Bryant was the one who had made him feel that way.

"I took the liberty of ordering you new clothes." Serihk spoke in his usual confident tone even as he dipped his chin instead of lifted it. "The ship's sensors had your measurements and I wanted to give you everything you need to move confidently and with authority in the circles I'll be bringing you into." The qesh took a deep breath and let it out again. "I apologize if that was an overbearing action on my part."

"Serihk." Bryant stepped close to the taller man and cupped his sharp jaw in his rough hands. A stroke of purple and pink brushed across Serihk's painfully pale face under Bryant's thumbs. "I'm the one that needs to apologize, not you."

Serihk shook his head and wrapped his long fingers around Bryant's wrists. "No, you don't—"

"I do." Bryant shook his own head harder. "All you've ever tried to do is help me and all I've ever done is thrown it back in your face."

Serihk drew Bryant closer to him. "You were scared."

"But I was cruel, too." Bryant pet his thumbs over the stripes of gray and purple that shimmered over Serihk's cheeks. "And I'm so sorry for that. I'm sorry I yelled at you. I'm sorry I pushed you away." Bryant swallowed. "I'm sorry I made you too nervous to even tell me you bought me new clothes."

Serihk sighed and gently pulled Bryant's hands from

his face so he could step around him and pick up the package. "That's not all on you."

"What do you mean?" Bryant accepted the package with a frown, surprised by its heft and curious to know what Serihk had picked out for him.

"I…" Serihk glanced up at the image of Oliver Turner and then at Bryant and he shook his head, orange snaking across the sides of his neck. "I can't keep trying to fix things I don't understand and then making them worse. I can't keep assuming I know better."

Bryant smiled crookedly and raised an eyebrow. "But you usually do know better."

That earned a deep chuckle from Serihk. "Not always. The candelabra, for instance?"

"I like the candelabra," Bryant admitted with a blush and loved the answering blush of purple that bloomed over Serihk's throat.

But then Serihk sighed. "Tava, for another. I'm beginning to think the peace deal I brokered was a mistake."

Bryant set the soft cloth package on the desk so he could cup Serihk's cheek again, reveling in the freedom to do so and in the way Serihk turned his nose into Bryant's palm. "Maybe it was, maybe it wasn't. But I'm going to be here helping you figure out what to do next for as long as you want me."

"And what if I want you forever?" Serihk whispered against the sensitive skin of Bryant's inner wrist. "Soft and safe?"

"Then I'll be here forever." Bryant slid his hand to the back of Serihk's head and tangled his fingers in his long soft hair. He pulled him down to kiss his lips gently, before saying, "But you can't promise me safety."

"I can." Serihk's dark eyes flashed with a challenging

stubbornness and Bryant smiled at the confident, sweet arrogance.

"You can't." Bryant chuckled and quickly kissed the next argument off of Serihk's lips. "But that's okay. I'm not afraid of that anymore."

Serihk sighed and finally brought his own hands up to Bryant's face. He rubbed his knuckles over Bryant's bearded jaw. "Are you afraid of something else?"

Bryant swallowed down the nerves in his throat that wanted to keep him from being vulnerable. Serihk had been vulnerable with him. He owed it to Serihk to be vulnerable, too. "Only that I'll be a bad partner for you."

Serihk gripped Bryant's jaw with a hard frown. "You won't. I'm certain of it."

Bryant huffed a laugh. "And who am I to argue with that?" He wished he had Serihk's confidence. After a beat, he gathered up what confidence he did have and finally asked the question that had been eating at him for hours. "Why did you put me in my own room?"

Embarrassed orange licked along the tips of Serihk's ears. "Because I'm trying to not be overbearing. Because I wanted to give you space."

Bryant bit down the retort that he didn't want space. It wasn't about what he wanted. He stepped close enough to feel the tall line of Serihk's body just a hairsbreadth from his own. "Do you want space?"

"No." Serihk tightened his grip on Bryant's jaw. Purple flowed up over his throat and jaw. "Goddess, no, I don't want any space at all."

Bryant's heart leaped in his chest and the guilty tide finally receded. He surged forward to feel Serihk's elegant body against his own again and relished Serihk's satisfied groan. Bryant pressed their foreheads together. "Then I'm moving in."

Bryant would move into Serihk's room, into his life, and into his heart and he was going to make damn sure he deserved to be there.

---

THANKS FOR READING The Alien Emissary!

MEET OLIVER TURNER of the dreaded Turner family and his own alien lover, Captain Mal'ik, in Book 2: The Alien Bodyguard!

# The Alien Refugee

GET this FREE short story exclusively available to those on my newsletter.

**HE'D SCOUR out his entire being if he knew any prayers with the power to do so.**

More than twenty years before the events of **The Alien Emissary** and a few short years after the brutal Klah'Eel invasion of Southern Tava, refugees of all kinds work to build new lives for themselves on the tropical planet of Carta.

Ha'ral came to Carta fleeing the horrors of the war – both the horrors that he witnessed and the horrors that he inflicted. He became a guard and dedicated himself to becoming a new man. A patient man. A kind man. A man who would never raise a hand in anger.

Maybe even a man who might deserve the playful smiles and casually intimate touches of the handsome human pickpocket who hangs around his patrols.

But Zyk came to Carta fleeing horrors of his own and

finding out who Ha'ral used to be might be more than Zyk can bear.

A *very* steamy 20k word short story set in the Inter-species Alliances world featuring a man yearning to be better, a man yearning to heal, and a happily ever after.

*Content Warning for on page violence and implied past sexual trauma.*

## About the Author

Eryn Ivers writes sci-fi and fantasy erotic romances about flawed men who have hot sex, feel too many things, and eventually live happily ever after.

She lives on the coast of California with her ridiculously lawful-good husband and chaotic-neutral cat.

Find her at erynivers.com, or sign up for her mailing list where you can receive exclusive offers, cover reveals, and book recommendations.

## Also by Eryn Ivers